When Worlds Collide
Ashlynn Carter

Copyright © 2024 by Ashlynn Carter

All rights reserved.

No part of this publication may be reproduced, distributed, or transmitted in any form or by any means, including photocopying, recording, or other electronic or mechanical methods, without the prior written permission of the publisher, except as permitted by U.S. copyright law. For permission requests, contact Ashlynn Carter at ashlynn.carter@proton.me.

The story, all names, characters, and incidents portrayed in this production are fictitious. No identification with actual persons (living or deceased), places, buildings, and products is intended or should be inferred.

Book Cover by Ashlynn Carter

First edition 2024

Chapter 1

Morgan Elliot finally finished scrubbing the last dog kennel before she quickly put the cleaning supplies away in the nearby closet and washed her hands. She needed to hurry. Pumba's crying and howling could be heard all the way from the side yard. The poor guy hated to be away from Timon and had been howling the whole ten minutes he was outside.

Morgan grabbed a slip lead off the hook and headed for the side door. As soon as she opened it, the little Jack Russel Terrier bolted inside. She laughed and followed Pumba back through the building. She had a pretty good idea of where he was going. Sure enough, Morgan found him jumping up and down in front of Timon's kennel.

"You were outside for only ten minutes, Pumba." Morgan scolded the dog with a smile as she picked him up and kissed his head.

Morgan loved working at the shelter in this small town. She had worked hard and earned her bachelor's degree in animal behavior. Her dream had always been to work with animals, dogs specifically.

After the accident, Morgan needed to get away from everything. Maple Grove provided her with the escape she needed and the opportunity to work with countless dogs while staying close to the city and Sally.

The animal shelter wasn't very big. It only had ten large kennels and six smaller ones they used for cats. There were always dogs to work with and she loved her boss. The saddest part about the shelter was that the dog kennels were constantly full.

Morgan had been there for two months, and she had yet to see an empty kennel for more than a day. People drove out to this area all the time just to dump the dogs they no longer wanted into the dense forest. Missy

Larson, the shelter's owner, constantly complained about the 'inhumane humans' and their disregard for life. Morgan wholeheartedly agreed with her.

The bell on the front door rang, and raised voices reached Morgan all the way in the back. She quickly put Pumba in his kennel and hurried to the front lobby to see what was happening. Chaos. That is the word she would use to describe the scene in front of her.

A large dog was thrashing on one end of a catch pole while a police officer was being jerked around on the other end. Missy was yelling at a man for running over the dog while two other men yelled at each other as they were trying to get the dog to hold still.

Morgan let out a loud whistle causing everyone to stop and look at her. The dog continued to growl, but his thrashing calmed to hard tugs against the catch pole. "What is going on?" Morgan asked.

"I *accidentally* hit the dog. It just ran out in front of my truck. I didn't have time to stop. I thought I killed it but then it woke up and started trying to bite everyone. I think it has rabies or something." Jake explained. He was a local, born and raised. He worked for his family's lumber business.

"If the dog was hit by a truck, why isn't he being taken to the vet?" Morgan asked as she stepped closer to examine the poor creature.

The dog stopped thrashing for a moment and Morgan noticed that a muzzle had been put on him. He looked at her with blue terror-filled eyes. That was no dog. The body shape alone told her that it was a wolf. The eyes, however, told her that this wolf wasn't just a wolf.

Morgan's childhood friend, Hailey Knight, turned out to be a werewolf. They were having a sleepover in Hailey's backyard when they were sixteen. Hailey ended up shifting for the first time in the middle of the night.

Both girls had been terrified about what had happened. The eyes of Hailey's wolf were the same as this wolf's. They shone with a higher intelligence than a wild animal was capable of. Morgan had learned a lot from Hailey about werewolves. Morgan's parents found out about the Knights and moved the whole family across the country.

"He is only going to hurt himself more if we can't calm him down." Missy stated.

"He is a danger to the community. It would be better to euthanize that beast." The Sheriff shot back as he struggled with the pole.

"I should be the judge of that." Morgan said through clenched teeth. There was no way she was going to allow these men to hurt this wolf; well, werewolf.

The Sheriff glared over at her. "What makes you so special?"

"Morgan is my animal behaviorist. She would know if the dog were dangerous or just acting out of fear." Missy informed the man before turning her attention to Morgan. "Where should we put him?"

"I just finished cleaning Pumba's kennel. We can move Pumba in with Timon and put this guy in the empty kennel." Morgan suggested.

Missy hurried through the door that led to the kennels to make space for the wolf. Morgan slowly approached the frightened creature. "It's okay, buddy." She talked soothingly to him.

Missy came running back in and told the group to follow her. Morgan cringed as she watched the three men practically wrestling the injured and scared werewolf into Pumba's old kennel. As soon as the gate was closed, the wolf cowered in the far back corner and growled at them.

"I still think we should have put a bullet in his head." Jake said under his breath.

"That is no dog. It has to be a werewolf." His friend, Devon, spat in the wolf's direction.

"That is most certainly a dog." Missy corrected. "I would say a Husky or Malamute mix. Wouldn't you agree, Morgan?"

All eyes turned to her, including the wolf's. "Absolutely. That dog is way too small to be a werewolf or even a normal wolf." Morgan pulled her eyes from him and looked at Jake. "And what is wrong with you? Who hits a dog?"

"It literally ran out of the forest and straight into the road." Jake said defensively. There was something in his expression that had Morgan's protectiveness rising. This was not an accident. Jake had intentionally hurt this werewolf. She was willing to bet anything that Jake and Devon hit the wolf on purpose.

"If that thing is a werewolf, let the sheriff's office know." The Sheriff said gravely. "They are extremely dangerous, and I don't want you girls getting hurt."

"Of course. If this dog proves to be a threat, we will take the proper precautions and notify those who need to know." Missy smiled at the Sheriff as she gestured for the men to head for the lobby. As soon as the Sheriff's back was turned, Missy rolled her eyes and made a face that had Morgan biting her lip to keep from laughing.

Morgan stayed back as she watched the others leave. She didn't understand why people were so scared of werewolves. Werewolves were just as common as humans were and no more dangerous than them either. Some lived in cities and mingled with the human population on a daily basis, while others lived in small towns that Hailey called packs. They had families and jobs just like humans did.

Once she was alone, Morgan turned her attention back to the wolf. The wolf was definitely on the smaller side, just like Hailey had been. He couldn't be more than sixteen.

Morgan learned that werewolves could shift to their wolf form for the first time anywhere between sixteen and eighteen years old. Those that shifted closer to sixteen tended to be on the smaller side for a few years.

"You're going to be okay." Morgan whispered as she opened the gate. She slowly slipped inside, not wanting to scare him anymore than he already was. "If you hold still, I can get that muzzle off of you." She kept her voice low as she made eye contact.

Normally, she would never make eye contact with a frightened dog. It was seen as a sign of aggression, but Morgan wanted the werewolf to see her sincerity. She sat on the floor near the gate and waited for any sign that he was going to let her remove the muzzle.

"What are you doing in there?" Missy gasped when she saw Morgan in the kennel.

"I am going to remove the muzzle." Morgan said calmly as she looked up at her friend.

Missy glanced over her shoulder before lowering her voice. "That is a wild animal, Morgan. Not a normal domesticated dog that was abandoned in the woods."

"I am aware of that fact." Morgan laughed as she scooted a little closer to the wolf. He growled and pressed himself deeper into the corner.

"I refuse to pay for any workman's comp you need after trying to get that muzzle off." Missy hissed.

Morgan smiled at Missy. "I wouldn't have it any other way. When I am done here, I will help you unload the dog food." Missy sighed in resignation before she left to start unloading the food.

Morgan had loaned Missy her truck to run to the neighboring town to pick up more dog food for the shelter. It was just past five o'clock and they needed to get the food brought in before they could go home for the day.

Morgan turned her attention back to the wolf. She watched him for another minute. She reached her hand out to unhook the clasp at the back of his head. The wolf attempted to snap at her as he growled more aggressively. Morgan raised her brow in challenge.

"Listen, young man. If you insist on acting like a wild animal, I will have to treat you like a wild animal. And believe me, you will not like how I get that muzzle off if we go down that road. Or you can just hold still for a few seconds, and I can get it off of you and you can sulk more comfortably. The choice is yours."

The wolf blinked at her as if surprised. She waited for a few more seconds before trying to unhook the muzzle again. This time the wolf didn't move. Morgan smiled at him as she slowly slid the muzzle off his face.

"See? Wasn't that easier than losing a wrestling match with me?" Morgan asked as she got to her feet. The wolf sneezed and shook his head. "Oh, I sure would have won. Then you would have had to go back to your pack and tell them all about the human girl who beat you up."

Morgan closed the gate behind her as she stepped out of the kennel. She looked back at the wolf. He seemed to be less scared but continued to cower in the corner. There was curiosity in his eyes as he studied her.

"We need to come up with a name for him." Missy said as she walked back down the aisle with a bag of dog food on her shoulder.

"I already have the perfect one." Morgan continued to smile at the wolf. "Taz." He cocked his head to the side.

"Taz?" Missy paused next to Morgan and looked at the wolf. He pressed himself back into the corner and growled. "As in Tasmanian Devil?"

"It's perfect!" Morgan laughed. "He came in like a tornado and Tasmanian Devils are timid unless threatened, then they fight. Just like this guy."

Missy laughed as she continued to take the food to the storage room. "Taz, it is." She called over her shoulder. "Now help me with all this food."

"See you later, Taz." Morgan winked at him before she left to help Missy unload the truck.

Thirty minutes later, all fifty bags of dog food were in the storage room. Morgan entered Taz into the system as a Husky mix and printed off his info card. Missy locked up the front lobby and office, while Morgan returned to the kennels. She attached the info card to the clipboard on the kennel and stood back.

Taz was brown and white in the typical husky pattern. He continued to huddle in the back corner as he watched her closely. Morgan noticed blood on the floor near his back leg. Concerned, Morgan went to find Missy.

"Missy? I don't think Taz should be left alone tonight." Morgan said as she glanced back at the door that led to the kennels.

"I was actually going to say the same thing." Missy sighed as she sat behind the reception desk. "This town is full of paranoid and ignorant people. With the Sheriff, Jake, and Devon thinking Taz is a werewolf, I am worried the latter two might try to break in and hurt him."

"Are werewolves a problem in this area?" Morgan asked. She had not heard of any werewolf attacks in the whole two months she had been here.

Missy let out a humorless laugh. "Not for nearly a hundred years. There is a nearby pack, but no one really knows where it is. I personally don't care, but some people are terrified of them. There seems to be an unspoken rule that if you kill one as a wolf, it is fair game, but if you kill one when they are human, its murder. The local men seem to see it as an achievement to kill a werewolf."

"That's terrible!" Morgan shook her head in disbelief. "What are we going to do about Taz? We can't let them get to him."

"He is locked up in the shelter and shouldn't be in danger from the werewolf hunting idiots, but paranoia does funny things to people." Missy rubbed her tired eyes. "One of us could stay the night here."

"I'll do it." Morgan offered. "You go home to your family, and I will see you in the morning."

"Are you sure?" Missy asked uncertainly.

"Positive."

Morgan watched Missy walk out to her minivan and drive away. She made sure the door was locked and the alarm set before going to the supply closet for first-aid supplies. Taz had been struck by a car and was bleeding. He needed help.

Morgan opened the gate to his kennel and settled down on the floor before dropping her armload next to her. She waited for Taz to calm back down before looking at him.

"Alright Taz, it's just you and me. Let's take a look at that injured leg of yours." Morgan scooted closer, but he snapped at her hand. "Really? You are going to act like that?"

Taz growled and tucked his legs in close to his body. He looked at Morgan with guarded eyes. He seemed to want to trust her but was still scared. Morgan tried to touch him again with the same result.

"I just want to clean the cut and wipe the blood off." Morgan told him. He remained tense and defensive. She sighed and leaned back against the wall. She was exhausted from the night before. Morgan had had another nightmare that made her unable to go back to sleep.

She tried a different tactic to connect with Taz. "I know you are probably not scared at all." She tried for a sarcastic tone. "I mean being hit by a car, muzzled, dragged to an animal shelter, and caged up; yeah, none of that is terrifying at all."

It didn't come across like she had hoped as her chest tightened and her voice became airy. Morgan closed her eyes. She didn't realize that her PTSD would flare up just thinking about a car accident. She took several deep breaths trying to calm her erratically beating heart. It took several minutes before she felt like she could speak again.

"Crap happens, Taz. It doesn't matter who you are. If you are living a good honest life, making stupid decisions, or if you are a terrible person, life will eventually blow up in your face. It is what you do after the crap hits the fan that matters." Morgan kept her eyes closed as she fought the memories that assaulted her.

Chapter 2

Morgan screamed as she jolted awake. She looked around frantically. It took her a few seconds to register that she was lying on the floor of Taz's kennel instead of being trapped in the mangled remains of her car. She was drenched in sweat and breathing hard.

Shaking her head, she sat up and turned to see a wide-eyed Taz standing next to her. He whined softly as he watched her. Morgan pulled her knees to her chest as her tears began to fall. Taz sat on the ground next to her so that his body pressed against her side.

Morgan put her arm around him and buried her face in his scruff. They sat like that for a long time before her tears finally stopped. She sat back, wiped her face and gave Taz a wobbly smile.

"I'm sorry." She took a deep breath and whispered. "I guess I owe you some sort of explanation."

Taz whined and licked her hand. Morgan wrapped her arms around her knees and stared at the wall in front of her. She swallowed a few times before she found her voice.

"My sister, my fiancé, and I were on our way to our favorite spot to have pizza and celebrate. She had just finished a hard test and I had graduated." Morgan's voice was little more than a whisper. "We had the radio cranked up and were singing at the top of our lungs and laughing. It was dark. As we rounded a corner, a large SUV had crossed the center line and was in our lane. The driver swerved but it was too late. I don't remember everything, but I know our car flipped a few times and slammed into a tree."

Morgan squeezed her eyes closed. She had a hard time talking about the accident, even though it had been six months ago. Taz pressed his head into Morgan's shoulder, and she looked over at him. His eyes were filled with sadness and worry. She gave him a weak smile. That was the most Morgan had been able to tell anyone but the police.

Her therapist said that talking about the incident would help her come to terms with it, but Morgan found it hard to open up. After the initial report, she just couldn't bring herself to talk about it. It made it feel too final. Too real. Maybe because Taz was a wolf at the moment, she felt more comfortable telling him. Regardless, Morgan was struggling to finish the story. That is what Morgan struggled the most to accept.

"Morgan!" Missy yelled from the lobby, causing both Morgan and Taz to jump.

"Thanks for listening." Morgan whispered before pressing a kiss to his head and standing up. She slipped through the gate before calling back to Missy. "I'm in the kennels!" Missy came rushing in, out of breath. "What's going on?" Morgan asked in alarm.

"Jeff got a call from Jake ten minutes ago. He said they wanted him to give them the keys to the shelter. He told them that I wasn't home." Missy explained. "We need to get Taz out of here before they show up."

Morgan looked over at Taz before running to the hooks where the slip leads hung. She grabbed one and ran back. "Okay boy, I need you to be cooperative for me." She opened the kennel and put the leash around his neck. "I am going to take him to my cabin." Morgan told Missy, who nodded her agreement. "Put in the records that I either adopted him or that I am fostering him."

Missy ran for the office while Morgan tried to lead Taz down the aisle towards the employee entrance. His movements were slow and stiff. She looked back at him and saw he wasn't putting any weight on his back leg. Morgan bent down and lifted him with a grunt and walked outside.

She didn't know what time it was, but it was still dark. She hurried to her truck and put Taz down to dig her keys out of her pocket. Once the doors were unlocked, Morgan picked Taz back up and laid him on the back seat.

Seeing her basket of clean clothes from her trip to the laundromat the other day, Morgan dumped them over Taz, completely covering him. Once she was sure no one would see the wolf in her car, she closed the door. Three vehicles pulled into the parking lot causing Morgan's heart to accelerate its rhythm even more than it already was.

She walked back towards the animal shelter where the security cameras would be able to record her from multiple angles and waited. Jake, Devon, and three other guys climbed out of the vehicles. Two of them had bats, while another one held chains. Morgan's heart felt like it was a thoroughbred on a racetrack.

"We don't open until nine. You will just have to come back later." Morgan said when they were ten feet away. She forced herself to remain calm.

"We are here for the beast the Sheriff brought in yesterday." Jake took a step closer to her.

"You will have to wait until we are open and fill out an adoption application." Morgan smiled at him. "Sorry."

She turned to head back inside but only made it a few steps before she was grabbed from behind. She screamed and threw her head back as hard as she could, connecting with her assailant's nose. The arms around her loosened and Morgan broke free. She spun around to see Jake holding his bloody nose.

Devon stormed up to her and backhanded her across the face. She fell and pain shot through her arm as she hit the pavement. Her cheek stung where he had struck her. Devon stepped up to her side and delivered a swift kick. A whoosh of air escaped her lungs as she grabbed her ribs and curled into a ball, trying to protect herself.

Devon reached down to grab her, and Morgan kicked him in the groin as hard as she could. He cried out in pain as he collapsed to the ground beside her. Morgan scrambled to her feet, keeping her injured arm tucked to her side. It was the same arm that she had broken in the accident. The cast had only been taken off a month earlier after two surgeries and tons of physical therapy.

A shotgun went off and all heads snapped in its direction. Missy stood with the gun pointed at the men with a stoney expression on her face. Morgan quickly moved to Missy's side as she fought back tears.

"What is going on here?" Missy asked, her eyes flashing with anger.

"We want the beast from yesterday." Jake demanded as he headed in her direction.

Missy lifted the shotgun to her shoulder and aimed it right at Jake's chest. "Wanting something doesn't give you the right to attack someone or break laws, Jake."

Sirens sounded in the distance and the atmosphere in the parking lot became more tense. Morgan wasn't sure adding the Sheriff to the mix would be a good or bad thing. The man had seemed to side with Jake and Devon earlier.

A patrol car screeched to a stop in the parking lot with lights flashing. The Sheriff and a deputy stepped out with guns aimed at Morgan and Missy.

"What in the world is going on?" The Sheriff bellowed. "Missy, put the gun down before someone gets hurt."

Missy lowered the shotgun as she continued to glare at the men. "Sheriff, these men attacked Morgan. I was only protecting her."

Now that Missy had lowered her gun to the ground, the Sheriff looked around at the scene in front of him. Devon still moaned as he rolled back and forth on the ground, while Jake held his bloody nose. Morgan held her arm close to her chest and was shaking.

"What's going on, boys?" The Sheriff finally asked as he holstered his firearm. The deputy followed suit but kept an eye on Missy.

Morgan waited to hear what excuses Jake and Devon would come up with. Jake wiped blood off his face as he looked at the ground while the three men with the bats and chains avoided eye contact. Devon was starting to uncurl from the fetal position but still seemed unable to speak. Morgan took some satisfaction in watching him.

"They said they wanted the dog you brought in yesterday. I told them to come back when we were open and fill out an application." Morgan said in a small voice when no one seemed keen on answering the Sheriff's question. "I tried to go back inside, and Jake grabbed me." She rubbed her sore ribs.

"I came out to see what was taking Morgan so long and saw Devon hit her." Missy yelled.

The Sheriff and deputy began taking statements and photographed Morgan's injuries. She refused to go to the hospital. Taz was still in her truck, and she needed to get him away from here. After an hour, Morgan was free to go. Missy told her to take the next several days off as Morgan climbed into her truck and headed for home.

Forty minutes later, Morgan pulled into her detached garage and cut the engine. She was exhausted, her head pounded, her arm ached, and her ribs protested every movement she made. She slid out of the truck and opened the back door. Taz's head popped up out of the mess and she gave him a small smile.

"Come on, buddy. Let's go inside. You are going to have to walk in because I cannot carry you right now." Morgan watched Taz carefully jump down and limped towards the house. She unlocked the door and led the way in. "You can take the couch. Try to get some sleep. We can figure out what to do in the morning." She paused at the threshold of her room. "Taz, my room is off limits. For no reason are you allowed in. Do you understand?"

When the wolf gave a small nod, she stepped in and closed the door. As she got dressed for bed, she looked at her injuries. She had multiple scrapes and bruises along her arm. Her left cheek was red and puffy. Now that the adrenaline was wearing off, her whole body ached.

Sighing, Morgan climbed into bed and snuggled under her blankets. She could not believe they attacked her because she told them to come back after the shelter opened. Missy was right, paranoia made people do crazy things. Morgan was just glad that Missy had come outside when she had, and that Taz was safe for the time being.

*   *   *

Morning came and Morgan groaned as she rolled over and got out of bed. She looked down at her arm and scrunched her nose. The skin looked even more raw than the night before. She jumped in a quick shower and made sure to clean the wounds thoroughly.

Looking in the mirror, she noted the swelling on her cheek. Sighing, Morgan exited her room and headed for the kitchen. She pulled out a bowl, cereal, and the milk, and set them on the table. She nearly screamed when she turned around and saw Taz sitting in the doorway of the kitchen watching her. She had forgotten she wasn't alone in the house.

"Geez, Taz. You gave me a heart attack." He cocked his head. "I bet you are hungry as well." Morgan returned to the cupboard and grabbed another bowl.

She poured a large bowl of Cheerios, added the milk, and set it on the floor. Taz trotted over to it and began devouring the food. Morgan laughed as she poured her own bowl of cereal. While she ate, she studied Taz. His limp seemed to be mostly gone and he didn't seem scared. He finished eating and stared at her expectantly.

"You know, if you shifted back to a human, you could get your own food." Morgan lifted her eyebrow and waited. Taz's tail wagged, but he didn't move. "Fine." Morgan sighed as she stood and poured him another bowl. "You owe me though."

Morgan spent the morning cleaning up the house. She noticed that Taz watched her closely from where he lay on the couch. Every wince or gasp of pain she made, caused his ears to stand straight up and he seemed more upset each time. After lunch, Morgan started to rip the boards off the back porch. She was planning on getting the deck replaced before Sally came home.

Her phone rang and she pulled it from her pocket. "Hello?"

"Ms. Elliot?"

"Yes." Morgan set her hammer down and stretched her legs out in front of her as she sat on the ground.

"This is Evangeline Winters." The older woman said, and Morgan smiled. She knew who was calling. She had saved her landlord's number in her phone when she signed the rental agreement. Not to mention the fact that the older woman called weekly to ask the same question.

"What can I do for you, Eva?"

"Well, I was just wondering how you were liking the cabin. You have been there for several months now." Evangeline was anything but subtle in her attempts to get Morgan to purchase the cabin instead of renting it.

"I love the cabin." Morgan began slowly. "I have been putting a lot of thought into your offer, and it's way too generous." Morgan stared out over the dense green forest around her. "Just the acreage alone is worth more than what you are asking."

"I am seventy-eight years old, Ms. Elliot. I don't have the time nor energy to keep up the property anymore. The four hundred acres of forest is unusable except for hiking, which is hardly worth anything. You would be doing me a favor by taking the property off my hands." Eva begged.

Morgan bit her lip as she surveyed the cabin and land from where she sat. She really did love this place. She enjoyed that Maple Grove was close enough to get to in thirty minutes but far enough away to allow her privacy. Sally would love it here, too.

"Okay." Morgan finally said. "When did you want to close?"

Morgan pulled the phone from her ear as Eva squealed in delight. Morgan couldn't help the laugh that bubbled up. She had never heard an old lady squeal before. "I will have my people get on the paperwork today. Would you like to close in two weeks? Is that too soon?"

"Two weeks sounds great." Morgan got to her feet and brushed the dirt from the seat of her pants.

"See you soon, dear."

Morgan stared at the phone for a long moment. If she signed the papers, she would be putting roots down here. She would be taking her first major step in moving on. The question was, was she ready?

Morgan dialed the clinic's number and followed the prompts to type in the right extension. Now that she had made a decision, she needed to let Sally know.

"Hello?"

"Hey, sis."

"Morgan!" Sally said excitedly. "What's up? I didn't expect to hear from you until tonight."

"I just got off the phone with Evangeline Winters." Morgan sighed as she laid on her back in the grass.

Sally laughed. "Did she ask you to buy the cabin again?"

Morgan smiled too. "Every time."

"Then why does it sound like this time was different?" Sally asked. Morgan closed her eyes. She missed her sister. Sally knew her better than she knew herself.

"Because it was." Morgan sighed. "I agreed to purchase the cabin and all four hundred acres."

Silence. Then came Sally's tentative voice. "Are you sure? That would mean making a commitment to Maple Grove and moving on."

"I know." Morgan whispered before taking a deep breath. "I think it might be time to let the past go."

"I'm proud of you, sis. I can't wait to see it." Sally's voice was quiet and full of hope, and Morgan fought the tears that threatened to fall. "You are still planning on calling tonight, right?"

"Of course I will." Morgan wiped her cheeks and nudged a rock with her toe. "Same time as always, Sal. I love you."

"Love you, too."

Morgan took a few cleansing breaths of the fresh air before heading back inside. When she opened the door, Taz was looking at her. She gave him a forced smile as she headed to her room. Morgan needed to have a few minutes alone. No match-making mamas, no injured wolves, no Missy.

She grabbed her motorcycle helmet and leather jacket and walked back into the living room. Seeing her gear, Taz sat up. The look in his eyes seemed to ask her where she was going.

"I am going out for a while. Stay here and don't let anyone inside. If anyone comes, hide in the attic." Morgan instructed as she walked out the backdoor without a backward glance.

Chapter 3

Morgan sat at the counter of the local bar. Fred handed her a second bottle of Dr. Pepper. She gave him a thankful smile. Fred patted her hand before continuing to wipe down the bar.

Morgan had tried to go to the diner, but Maive was working. Maive was super nice, but she constantly tried to get Morgan to go out with her son, Eli. He wasn't necessarily a bad guy, but Morgan had no interest in him.

Morgan took a long drink, enjoying the fizz of the carbonation as it burned her throat. She had never tasted a drop of alcohol before the accident, and she never would now. Being hit by a drunk driver will do that to a person; remove all desire for the stuff.

The bar down the road had been where Morgan went when she was trying to hide from everyone. The problem with tonight was that Eli was passed out drunk at the other end of the counter. It was barely four o'clock. Morgan shook her head. Yeah, she wasn't going to be getting involved with Eli anytime soon.

Morgan closed her eyes as she listened to the music and played with the almost empty soda bottle in her hands. A warm hand touched her thigh as rancid breath puffed into her face. She opened her eyes to see Eli sitting on the bar stool next to her.

She resisted the urge to lean away from him. She would not show him that he affected her. Morgan grabbed his hand and removed it from her leg. Eli scowled at her.

"Oh, come on, sweetheart. You know we belong together." Eli whined.

"The answer is, no, Eli." Morgan rolled her eyes as she looked forward and took the last drink of her soda.

"Don't be like this." Eli leaned closer to her just as an arm came around her shoulders from the other side.

Morgan whipped around in her seat to see who it was. This was all she needed right now, two drunk men demanding her attention.

A man she had never seen before stood beside her. "Hey, Baby. Sorry I'm late. Work ran later than I had planned." The man said as he leaned in for a kiss.

Morgan leaned back as she placed a hand on his chest to stop him. They were so close that their noses were touching. The man had beautiful blue eyes with flecks of brown in them. His eyes flicked to Eli before returning back to her. He seemed to be asking if she needed help.

Deciding to use the guy as a means to get away from the intoxicated nuisance next to her without causing a big scene, Morgan smiled. "Sorry, you have to work a little harder to get some of that." Morgan said softly.

"I would be willing to work all night to get the job done." The stranger rubbed his nose against hers and Morgan's eyes widened before a laugh burst from her. The man's smile grew, but he didn't move any closer to her.

Morgan gently pushed on his chest as she stood. He took a step back to allow her to get up. She couldn't seem to pull her eyes away from his. She slowly ran her hands up and down his chest. She could feel his heart beating fast under her hand. The man's hand settled on her hip as he watched her. His eyes almost seemed to be darkening as they stood there studying one another.

Morgan knew she should move away from this man. She didn't even know who he was, but there was something about him that calmed her. She fought the urge to lean against him, even though something inside told her that she would be safe and protected with him.

"Morgan." Eli snapped as he grabbed her arm and yanked her away from the stranger. "How dare you allow some guy to touch you." He seethed.

A movement over Eli's shoulder drew her attention. Several men were watching her with ticked off expressions. Two were standing next to their table and looked ready to storm over to her. Eli's grip tightened and she turned back to him.

"Eli, I told you this several times, we are not going to happen. Now, let go." Morgan whispered harshly. She was done trying to let him down easy.

Eli opened his mouth as if to say something but was interrupted. "I strongly suggest you take your hands off my girl." The stranger warned. His voice was calm, but there was steel behind his words.

Eli's grip slackened and Morgan yanked her arm away from him. She took a step back and bumped into the stranger. She turned to him as she slipped her arms around his waist. His arm went around her back as he held her protectively. Eli's jaw ticked as he clenched it.

"You ready to go, Baby?" the stranger whispered close to her ear. Morgan nodded and stepped away from him. He moved so that he was between her and Eli as she slipped her leather jacket on.

Morgan turned to Fred who was watching her with an amused smile. "Thanks for the drinks, Fred." She gave him a smile and he waved in acknowledgement.

The stranger's arm went back around her, and she leaned into him. Eli glared at the man behind her. "Go home, Eli. Sober up." She said firmly before allowing herself to be guided outside.

As soon as they were a few steps away from the door, the stranger released his protective hold on her. Morgan glanced at him as he put his hands in his pockets. They walked slowly out into the parking lot. "Was that too much?" The man asked.

Morgan stopped walking and studied the man. He stood several inches taller than her, and Morgan was no more than half his size. His hair was a rich brown and long enough to fall over his ears and into his eyes. It was messy as if he had been wearing a hat or helmet recently. He had a strong jawline that had a few days' worth of scruff. His shirt pulled tight over his broad chest, making his athletic figure obvious to anyone who looked at him. His jeans hung low on his hips as he carried himself with confidence.

"Maybe a little." Morgan shrugged.

He looked up and gave her a small smile. "Can I walk you to your car?"

Morgan nodded and started to walk to her motorcycle that was parked on the other side of Fred's white sedan. "Eli isn't usually that bad." Morgan said softly.

"Maybe not, but he wasn't taking 'no' for an answer." The man glanced over at her.

"I'm not totally helpless." Morgan laughed while she slowed her steps as they approached Fred's car. The man slowed as well and looked at her.

"I never said you were, Baby." The man looked like he was trying not to laugh.

He tried to open the front door, but it was locked. He looked back at her with a raised brow. Morgan crossed her arms over her chest as she narrowed her eyes. She was trying to look offended that he didn't think she could protect herself but there was something charming about this guy.

"You fancy yourself my knight in shining armor?" Morgan asked.

The man turned to fully face her. He looked her up and down. "That depends on you, Baby. Do you want me to be?" he asked with a crooked grin. His gaze dropped to her cheek before lifting back to her eyes. His jaw tightened and Morgan's heart stuttered.

Morgan laughed as she shook her head. "Look, Wolf, I appreciate your assistance with Eli, but I am a big girl and can take care of myself."

"Wolf?" The man asked in surprise.

"Your shirt." Morgan gestured to his chest.

The man looked down at the logo on his chest and Morgan swung her leg over her motorcycle. Wolf looked back at her. His eyes widened in surprise before a lazy smile spread across his face. His gaze traveled over her appreciatively.

"You have a little drool right here." Morgan pointed to the corner of her mouth. She put on her helmet as she smiled. "I know this bike is stunning, but you should pull yourself together." Morgan gave a small shrug and Wolf laughed. "And it looks like your boys are looking for you."

A group of guys was standing by the bar's door watching them. When Wolf turned to look at the bar, Morgan started her bike. The engine roared to life and Wolf whipped his head back around to her.

"Baby, I need your name." Wolf said with a lopsided grin.

"What was that? I can't hear you!" Morgan yelled.

Wolf opened his mouth as if to speak and Morgan revved the engine. He smiled then tried again, but Morgan once again revved the engine, and his smile grew. He took a step toward her, and she let off the brake and shot forward. She wound her way through the parking lot as she headed for the exit.

She stopped at the road to look both ways. Something compelled her to look back to see Wolf's reaction. He still stood where she had left him. He watched her as his friends laughed and slapped his back. She blew a kiss before turning right and speeding out of town.

As she took the winding road up to the cabin, Morgan thought back on her interaction with Wolf. He was handsome and his corny lines made her laugh. It had been a long time since she had just let herself enjoy life in the moment.

She pulled into the detached garage and went inside the house. Taz greeted her with a bark and tail wag. Morgan tossed her helmet on her bed and pulled her jacket off. She plopped down on the couch with a sigh. Taz jumped up beside her and she looked at him.

"How was your evening?" she asked. Taz only watched her. "Mine was good until Eli started hitting on me again. Ugh." Morgan couldn't help the smile that split her face. "Then some guy came over and tried to pretend I was his girlfriend or something."

Taz sniffed her and cocked his head to the side. He whined softly as he looked outside. "I know, buddy. As soon as you are better, I will drive you wherever you need to go. Until then, you can be my bestie." Morgan patted his head before he climbed off the couch and went outside.

Morgan's phone rang and she looked at it. Smiling, she answered the phone. "You are late." Sally didn't waste any time reprimanding her.

"I was in town earlier. I literally just got home." Morgan defended herself.

"Why do you sound like you are smiling?" Sally asked in surprise.

"I smile." Morgan shook her head.

"Not really. Not the kind that effects your voice." Sally stated. "I've missed it." There was a pause. "So, what happened to make you so happy?"

"How was PT? How are the crutches coming?" Morgan deflected.

"PT is brutal. But I have been doing so good that they are talking about graduating me to crutches." Sally said excitedly.

"That's great!" Morgan sat up straighter. "They said you could be released once you didn't need the wheelchair anymore."

"I want out of here so bad. I miss you." Sally's voice took on a sad tone.

"I miss you too. Keep working hard. I was planning on picking up furniture for your room this weekend when I come to visit. Any preference on paint color?"

Morgan closed her eyes against the pain of not having her sister with her. Morgan and Sally were nine years apart. Morgan had become Sally's legal guardian when their parents died in a boating accident four years ago. Sally had been only ten at the time and Morgan nineteen.

The two were incredibly close. The car accident nearly cost Morgan everything she held dear in life. Sally had severely broken her leg. After surgery, she required extensive physical therapy. Morgan only had a broken arm and had a long piece of scrap metal removed from her abdomen. Morgan's fiancé, Luke, died.

It was at Luke's funeral that Morgan learned that he had been cheating on her. Two months after the accident the police asked about Luke's drug use. He had been under the influence when the drunk driver hit them. She had no idea that he even used them. Not only did she mourn the loss of the man she thought she loved, but also had to process his betrayal.

"I would be happy with anything with color. I am so tired of white." Sally sighed dramatically.

Morgan laughed. "Would you like me to bring you something to spruce up your space?"

"Yes." Sally cried. "And something edible. I'm dying here, Morgan. Please take me home this weekend."

"I wish I could, Love." Morgan's heart broke for her sister. "You keep working with the crutches and you will spring free of that place in no time."

"Do you know what will cheer me up?"

"What?" Morgan was instantly on guard. She practically raised her sister and knew that tone.

"You telling me what has you so happy."

Morgan laughed. "Okay, okay."

She got up off the couch and headed for her room. She closed the door, walked into the bathroom, and started the shower before sitting on the floor. Hailey had told her that werewolf hearing was crazy good, and she didn't want Taz listening in on her.

Morgan told Sally all about going to the bar and Eli's advances. Sally laughed when Morgan told her about Wolf coming to the rescue and her response. Giggling came from Sally's end of the phone as Morgan finished with blowing a kiss and riding off.

"He sounds so cute. I can't believe you were flirting with him." Sally giggled.

"I wasn't flirting with him." Morgan shot back. "I am not ready for a relationship. Luke..."

"Luke is gone, Morgan. You deserve to be happy. Flirting does not mean you have to be in a relationship with this guy. Just pretend not to be old and enjoy life."

Morgan laughed. "I will see you in two days young lady. Stay out of trouble until I get there and can cause it with you."

They said goodnight and Morgan smiled down at her phone. She was glad that Luke was no longer in her life. Guilt washed over her. She felt bad that he was dead, but at the same time, she was so glad that she learned of his addiction and several girlfriends before they were married.

The funeral had been enlightening when three women came up to her and introduced themselves to her. They had been seeing Luke the whole time Morgan was in a relationship with him. They told her that Luke had kept his relationship with them strictly physical. Apparently, he complained to them that Morgan wasn't willing to take that step until after they were married, so he had to go find it somewhere else.

Morgan had been mortified. She had been so blind. She vowed to never be in that situation again. All she needed was Sally and maybe a dog or two. Dogs were loyal and loved unconditionally.

Morgan headed back out to the front room. Taz jumped off the couch when she sat down. He brought her the remote and she smiled before putting on an action movie.

Chapter 4

Morgan stretched. She looked around. She had fallen asleep on the couch with Taz. He stretched and yawned. Morgan got up and made breakfast. After clearing the dishes, she turned to Taz.

"I know that werewolves have faster healing than humans, but I'm not sure how long you need to get better." Morgan watched Taz for any sign of the answers she was wanting but found none. "I need to go to work so you will be here on your own again. I should be back by six. If you need anything, call the animal shelter, the number is on the fridge."

Morgan took a quick shower before getting on her motorcycle and heading back into Maple Grove. She groaned when she pulled into the shelter's parking lot and saw Devon's jeep. Morgan slipped in through the back door and started cleaning kennels.

"There you are." Missy's voice startled Morgan as she put Timon and Pumba back into their kennel. So much for hiding out until they left, she had only been there for ten minutes.

"Yeah, I came in the back." Morgan glanced at her boss.

"Devon and Jake aren't happy that you adopted the husky." Missy made a small gesture with her hand and Morgan knew they were close by.

"The husky is extremely fearful." Morgan stated.

"I know, that is why I allowed the most qualified person to adopt him. You have the training to handle such a special case." Missy said loudly.

"That's bull." Jake growled as he came around the corner. "That beast is dangerous."

Diesel started barking as he lunged forward, slamming hard against the gate. The Doberman had a thing about guys. Morgan had been working with him for the past two weeks, but his progress was slow going. He was one of Morgan's favorites here at the shelter.

"Why don't we take this conversation somewhere else." Morgan suggested in a loud voice in order to be heard over Diesel's barking, as she headed for the lobby.

Once they were able to hear each other, Missy moved to Morgan's side. "Morgan has legally adopted the husky. He belongs to her."

"Can we talk about this?" Devon asked, looking at Morgan.

"Could I take my lunch now and go to the diner to talk with them about everything that is required for the husky?" Morgan turned to Missy for permission. Secretly she hoped that Missy would say Morgan was needed here.

Missy grudgingly nodded her head and Morgan walked outside with Jake and Devon. They remained silent as they walked down the sidewalk. The diner was a quarter mile down the road, but with Devon and Jake walking behind her, it felt longer. Morgan's anxiety climbed with each step she took.

The bell chimed as they stepped inside. Morgan walked to the back corner booth. It was the largest booth in the place and farthest from the door. She hadn't been thinking when she chose this seat. It was her normal spot and she had just automatically moved to it. Now that they were seated, Morgan wished they were at a more public table.

Maive approached their table with a smile on her face. "What can I get started for you?"

"Water with a lemon please." Morgan answered while keeping a close eye on the two men across from her.

They ordered their coffees, then waited for Maive to give them their menus and to leave before they focused on Morgan. Morgan remembered clearly what had happened the last time they had encountered one another. Her face was still slightly swollen, her arm was all scraped up and her ribs were bruised. Jake had two black eyes and bruising all around his nose.

"We want the dog, Morgan." Jake said in a low threatening voice.

"Are you aware of the time and energy it takes to care for a husky?" She asked. "Especially one that is extremely fearful?"

"Here you go." Maive returned and placed their drinks on the table. "Do you know what you want to eat?"

"Can we have a few more minutes, Maive?" Morgan gave the woman a forced smile.

Maive nodded and hurried away as the bell above the door rang again. Morgan's back was to the door so she couldn't see who it was, but she felt eyes on her. She took a sip of her water. Jake's eyes shifted to just over Morgan's shoulder and she tensed, prepared for Eli to slide into the booth beside her.

"Hey, Baby." The deep voice caused Morgan's head to snap up.

She let out a tense breath and smiled. "Hey, yourself."

Wolf slid in next to her. His arm rested on the back of the booth behind her. He leaned in so that his lips were right next to her ear, and she turned her head towards him causing their cheeks to brush.

"Everything okay?" He whispered. Morgan relaxed a little more, leaning against him. She had no idea why this man's presence made her feel safer. Wolf pulled her closer to him. "I take that as a no." He pressed a quick kiss to her temple.

He pulled back and looked at her face. His eyes once again settled briefly on her swollen cheek. "Are you going to tell me who hit you?" He asked loud enough for those around them to hear.

"There was a wolf attack at the animal shelter a few nights ago." Devon said and Morgan stiffened.

Her jaw clenched as she glared at Devon. "If by a wolf attack you mean five men threatening to break into the animal shelter, then sure we can go with that."

Wolf's arm around her tensed. She looked up at his face. He was looking between the three of them as if trying to understand what was going on.

Jake cleared his throat. "Who's your friend, Morgan? I don't think I have seen him around before."

"I thought you wanted to talk about the husky?" Morgan clenched her hands under the table. She couldn't believe these two. "I asked you a question, Jake. Do you or do you not know how to properly take care of a husky: their level of energy, food requirements, grooming, exercise, their social needs?"

"We don't need to know any of that." Devon shot back at her. "You should have just given him to us the other night, but instead you had to be difficult."

"Difficult?" Morgan bristled. "You haven't even begun to see difficult."

Wolf's hand started to rub up and down her arm in a soothing motion. If she wasn't so tense, she might have leaned against him again. Devon slammed his fist on the table.

"Come on, Baby. Let's get you out of here." Wolf stood and offered her his hand. She took it and got to her feet.

"This conversation isn't over yet." Jake called after them as they began to head for the door. Morgan started to turn around, ready to smack the smirk off his bruised face.

Wolf put his arm around her and guided her outside. She let out a huff of frustration and pulled away from Wolf. He didn't try to touch her again as she walked down the sidewalk back to the shelter. She opened and closed her fist several times until a large hand slipped into hers.

Wolf pulled her to a stop in front of the shelter. "Baby, calm down."

Morgan's jaw tightened. "Did you just tell me to calm down?" She hated those words. Her father would always say that to her whenever she cried after he hit her, and Luke said it to her constantly when she got frustrated with him checking other girls out.

"To be honest, the moment those words came out of my mouth, I knew they were a mistake."

Morgan let out a long breath and closed her eyes. Her shoulders sagged as her anger began to cool. Wolf was right, she did need to calm down. Her momma bear was on a war path again. The last time was when some of the other girls on Sally's cheer squad were bullying her. She just couldn't let anything happen to Taz. She needed to protect him.

Wolf's thumb gently ran over her knuckles as she felt him step closer. His other arm went around her, and she leaned forward. He released her hand and wrapped his arm around her. Morgan heard Sally's voice in her head telling her to enjoy life and she slowly raised her hands to rest them against Wolf's chest.

He held her for several minutes before pulling back and looking down at her. He ran his thumb softly over her cheek. "So, which one of those guys gave you this?"

Morgan sighed and stepped away. "The same one that kicked her in the ribs." Missy's voice caused Morgan to jump. "Who's this?"

"This is…Wolf." Morgan shrugged as a smile tugged at her lips as she remembered the other night.

"You're naming people now, too?" Missy shook her head. "Why don't you both come inside?"

"I couldn't very well call him 'that guy'." Morgan laughed as she followed Missy inside.

"You could have a conversation with a man and ask his name." Missy pointed out.

"I guess." Morgan scowled. She was aware that Wolf stood behind her, listening to the conversation.

"You have to talk with guys at some point, Morgan."

"I talk to boys all the time." Morgan crossed her arms over her chest.

"Dogs don't count and telling the human ones to 'buzz off' isn't a conversation." Missy laughed as she shook her finger at Morgan before looking at Wolf. "Now, you seem to be a decent man, what's your real name, Wolf?"

Wolf coughed as if trying to cover a laugh before clearing his throat. "My name is Maverick. Maverick Storm, ma'am."

Morgan whirled around. "Seriously?"

She stared at him in shock. Top Gun had been her favorite movie her whole childhood and she had the biggest crush on Maverick for most of her teen years. Morgan couldn't stop the laugh that burst from her. This guy just got better. Sally was going to love this.

"Is there something wrong with my name?" Maverick asked, putting his hands on his hips. His eyes twinkled with laughter, even though his jaw was set in a firm line.

"Of course not." Morgan smiled at him. "It's just, it's just..." Morgan shook her head as she looked over at Missy who looked at her like she had grown a third eye. "Oh gosh. I need a drink." Morgan laughed as she headed for the mini fridge behind the reception desk.

She turned back around as she put the bottle to her lips. Missy and Maverick were watching her. Maverick was smiling, while Missy looked shocked. The bell rang and Devon and Jake walked in. Morgan put the lid back on her soda and set it down. She moved around to stand by Missy.

"You two are not welcome in here." Missy stated.

"We are here to fill out an application for the Doberman." Devon said as he made eye contact with Morgan.

"You are not welcome here and you will not be permitted to adopt any of our animals." Missy stepped in front of Morgan to block Devon's view of her.

Maverick crossed his arms over his chest as he observed the other two men. "I think that means it is time for you to leave."

Morgan looked over at Maverick. He made an intimidating image standing with his feet slightly apart, pulling his tall muscular frame to its full height, and a 'don't mess with me' look on his face. Devon and Jake glared over at Morgan before turning and leaving.

"What is going on?" Maverick asked after they watched Jake and Devon drive away. He moved close to Morgan and touched her arm softly. He lifted it and looked at the scratches along her arm.

"We got a new dog two nights ago. Those two and three of their friends feel like the dog is a threat. Morgan was taking the dog somewhere to hide him for a few days, but they showed up before she could leave." Missy explained.

"So, they attacked you for taking the dog?" Maverick asked, his body radiating tension.

"No. We were closed, so when they approached me and demanded I hand the dog over, I told them to come back once we opened and fill out an application." Morgan closed her eyes as memories of the attack flooded her mind. She felt Maverick's arm go around her again. "Jake tried to grab me, and I broke his nose." Morgan whispered.

"I heard her scream and came out to see what was going on. Morgan was on the ground. Devon kicked her in the ribs before she dropped him with a kick of her own." Missy continued the story. "I told her to take a few days off, but here she is."

"Babe, why didn't you say something earlier?" Maverick's voice was just loud enough for her to hear.

"Maverick, its fine. I'm fine. Plus, I met you only yesterday. It's not like we are in any sort of relationship." Morgan looked up at him.

Tears blurred her vision. She had no idea why she was losing control of her emotions. She could usually hold the tears back until she was alone. But all she wanted to do was step back into Maverick's arms. Morgan dropped her gaze to the floor and blinked rapidly to stop the tears.

So much had happened over the past six months, and it all seemed to be rushing to the surface. She took a deep breath, and the soreness of her ribs reminded her of healing after the car accident. Her broken ribs had been brutal. She rubbed them as the memory of the car accident brought back the pains of Luke's betrayal. Everything slammed into her all at once and the dam broke.

Maverick pulled her to him and cradled her head as her tears fell. She vaguely heard Missy excuse herself as Morgan's tears turned to sobs. Morgan cried until she felt exhausted and sleepy. Maverick wiped her tears with his thumbs.

"I'm sorry." Morgan whispered as she tried to back away from Maverick. She was sure he thought her a complete psycho.

"You have nothing to be sorry for." Maverick kept his arms around her. "Now what would you like to do?"

"Honestly? Sleep." Morgan closed her eyes and sighed. "But there is no way I can drive home right now."

"I might have a solution to that."

Morgan stood just inside the room. Maverick had taken her to the hotel, handed her a key and told her the room number. He said he needed to meet up with his friends to get some work done, so she was free to use the room. Too tired to argue, Morgan relented.

She made sure the door was fully closed and locked before making her way to the bed. She pulled her shoes and jeans off before she climbed under the covers with a sigh. She didn't even remember her head hitting the pillow.

Chapter 5

Male voices roused Morgan from a deep sleep. She rolled over and buried her head under the blankets. The voices stopped. Morgan stiffened. Her heart rate accelerated as she realized she was not in her bed.

"Hey, Baby, you up?" Maverick's voice was soft.

Morgan lowered the blanket and sat up. She blinked several times as her eyes adjusted to the lights. Not only was Maverick sitting in the room but so were five other men.

"Really, Maverick?" Morgan crossed her arms over her chest as she glared at him. She was acutely aware that her jeans were somewhere on the floor.

"What?" Maverick asked confused.

"I need you all to leave." Morgan stated firmly, even though her heart was hammering nervously. "Now."

All six men looked between each other before all focus landed back on her. Morgan's mind was racing, trying to figure out a way to locate her pants and get out of this hotel when six very large, very intimidating men stood between her and the exit.

Morgan went with her "Momma Bear" voice as Sally calls it. "I said, now!"

All but Maverick got to their feet and beat a hasty retreat. Once the door closed, Maverick slowly stood before moving to the side of the bed and sitting down beside her.

"How are you feeling?" he asked.

"Like I want to rip your head off." Morgan shoved his shoulder. He laughed and got back to his feet. "When I said everyone out, I meant you too."

"This is my room." Maverick smirked.

"It may be your room, but I am currently in only my shirt and underwear." Morgan felt her cheeks flush. "I would like to get dressed without an audience."

Maverick's eyes widened in surprise. They both remained still for a long moment before Maverick walked quickly to the door and left. Morgan jumped from the bed the moment she heard the door click closed, and quickly located her pants. At least he was some sort of gentleman and stepped outside.

Morgan pulled her phone from her pocket and noticed she had eight missed calls from Sally. Panic built inside her as she dialed her sister's number with shaking hands. While she waited, she started pulling on her shoes.

"Hello?" Sally answered with a desperate tone in her voice.

"Sally? What's wrong?" Morgan asked quickly.

Sally broke down crying. "Where have you been? Why didn't you answer your phone?"

"I'm so sorry, Sally. I didn't hear it going off. What's wrong?" Morgan asked again.

"You didn't call me last night. I tried calling you, but you didn't answer. I thought something happened to you." Sally was sobbing now.

Guilt stabbed into Morgan's chest. How did she not hear her phone going off? She glanced at the clock on the bedside table. How could she have slept until ten the next day? Morgan ran for the door. All of the guys were in the hall waiting.

She shoved past them as she sprinted for the nearest elevator. "I'm on my way, Love. I will be there in an hour, okay? Everything is okay."

Morgan made it to the elevator and frantically started pushing the arrows. The darn thing was taking too long, so Morgan pushed open the door to the stairs. She heard running feet behind her, but she didn't look back.

Sally still hadn't answered Morgan by the time she reached the ground floor and sprinted outside. "I'm going to hang up now so I can drive, okay?"

Sally gave a small sound of confirmation before Morgan hung up the phone. Now that she was no longer talking on the phone, she ran faster down the road to the animal shelter. She bolted inside to grab her helmet and jacket before running to her bike.

Maverick and his crew were waiting by her motorcycle with confused and worried expressions. She didn't slow down as she approached them. Maverick moved to stand in her way and Morgan slid to a stop.

"What's going on, Baby?" he asked as he reached for her.

Morgan pushed her helmet into his hands so she could get her jacket on. "Look. I appreciate what you did for me yesterday, I really do. But I messed up big time and I need to fix things."

Maverick's expression hardened. "Your man is mad that you didn't come home last night?"

Morgan paused and looked up at Maverick. Her panic began fading as she studied him. "I will be fine." She bit the inside of her cheek to keep from smiling. Was he jealous?

"I don't think you should go alone." He insisted as Morgan grabbed her helmet from him.

"Suit up, Goose." Morgan said looking over at the man on Maverick's right. He was a foot taller than she was and had tattoos snaking up his neck. His bald head and thick beard made him look like a burly biker. In all honesty, he scared her. But she didn't have the time to be distracted by Maverick. "You are my wingman for the next hour."

The man's eyebrows shot up in surprise while Maverick scowled at her. Before she could put her helmet on, Maverick pulled her close to him. "That's not what I meant."

Morgan's heart rate accelerated at his closeness, and she resisted the urge to wrap her arms around his neck. His hold on her was tight, but she didn't feel threatened. He was kind of cute when he was being protective. "I hate to break it to you Maverick, but I only answer to one person and that person isn't you." She patted his chest and stepped back as she put her helmet on.

She climbed on her bike before glancing over as she started the engine. Morgan noticed that Goose was running back to the hotel while the others watched her. Maverick looked like he wanted to say more, but he remained silent. She gave them a salute before peeling out of the parking lot.

*   *   *

Maverick watched as Morgan disappeared down the road. She was driving fast, and he wasn't sure if Charlie would be able to catch up to her. He ran his hand through his hair in frustration. He should have insisted that he ride with her.

"We are just going to let her go?" Cole asked.

"We can't keep her hostage." Bentley scoffed.

Charlie whipped by on his bike and Maverick sighed. "Charlie will keep an eye on her."

Brett laughed. "I bet that grates on you, Mav. Having your girl request another in order to go see a different guy?"

Maverick clenched his fists and started walking back toward the hotel. He had not planned on finding his mate when he came to Maple Grove. They were there to locate his brother. Jayden had shifted for the first time only last month. Last week, he went for a run but never returned.

Mom and dad were beside themselves with worry and Maverick volunteered to find him. Their whole pack knew that Maple Grove was off limits. The people there tended to shoot first and ask questions later.

Maverick and the others followed Jayden's scent to the small town. It led them to a bar. After entering, Maverick had spotted a woman sitting at the bar counter. A man was obviously not taking the hint to back off, so Maverick decided to help the woman out.

The moment the woman turned to face him, and they touched, he immediately recognized her as his mate. His wolf, Timber, howled in excitement, but she didn't seem to feel the mate bond. Timber couldn't seem to sense her wolf and told him that she was human. The bond was much weaker for her because she was not a werewolf. It was rare that a werewolf had a human mate, because they were unable to have kids. The last human-werewolf mate pair he knew of was several hundred years ago.

Maverick reached his room and slammed the door shut. He needed to calm down. Morgan was his mate, and he would fight for her to the very end. Just because she was in a relationship now, didn't mean she couldn't change her mind.

Maverick glanced over at the bed. The covers were thrown back and there was a sock on the sheets. He picked it up with a small smile, but it faded fast. She had been in such a rush that she hadn't realized she was missing a sock. He sat on the bed and ran a hand through his hair. Morgan was wreaking havoc on his life, and he had only known her for a day or two.

He had fully expected to come back to an empty room when he returned late last night. To his surprise, Morgan was still asleep in the bed. He lay on the couch, not wanting her to feel threatened by him in any way. She started tossing and turning in her sleep. Maverick tried to wake her up. She sat up crying, but didn't seem to be fully awake. He was desperate to help soothe her.

Maverick sat next to her and held her. Morgan wrapped her arms around him, clinging to him as she buried her face in his chest. She quickly fell back to sleep, and he continued to hold her for a little while longer. Something traumatic had to have happened to her for her to be acting like this. He could feel it. Maverick wished he could take it away.

Every time he got up and moved back to the couch, Morgan would become restless again. He would move back to the bed, and she would calm down when she felt him near. He decided to stay in the bed, so she could get the sleep she needed. She clung to him when he laid down and pulled her close to him. Maverick ended up holding her for hours as she slept. Only when there was a knock on the door did he finally get up.

He wanted to ignore whoever it was but knew that if Morgan woke and found him in bed with her, even if he was on top of the covers, she would be angry. Morgan was right, they were practically strangers. Hopefully, not for much longer. He was determined to get to know his intriguing mate.

A knock on his door pulled him from his thoughts. Brett, Bentley, Hank, and Colt were standing there. "What?" Maverick snapped.

"Can we come in?" Hank asked, his voice was deep, and he talked with a slow southern drawl.

Maverick stepped back and allowed the guys back in. "What is it?" he asked again, once the door was closed.

"Jay's scent is fainter now than it has been since we got here." Colt answered.

"It is strongest at the animal shelter and the diner. There are even faint traces here at the hotel." Bentley added.

Maverick ran a hand down his face. Jayden's scent hit his nose. He looked down at his hand before sniffing it. His brother's scent. Maverick looked around and saw the sock he had dropped back on the bed. He lifted it to his nose. Jayden's scent was mixed with Morgan's.

"Whose sock is that?" Hank asked, stepping closer to him. "It smells like Jay."

"It's Morgan's." Maverick stated.

"She is the key to finding Jayden." Colt said. "We need to keep a close eye on her; she could lead us to him."

*   *   *

Morgan tapped her toe impatiently as she waited for her tank to fill up. She was less than five miles from the clinic, but her fuel gauge was reading empty. She was anxious to get to Sally. She couldn't even imagine the terror her sister was living through last night while Morgan slept soundly.

Guilt once again filled her. Their parents' boating accident had left both Sally and Morgan with scars. They suffered panic attacks when they couldn't get ahold of each other. Their parents were not the best, but their sudden absence had been shocking. Morgan and Sally had become aware of how quickly a life could be taken. Their car accident six months ago only added to their anxiety.

A motorcycle pulled up beside her. She recognized the rider once he removed his helmet. "You can fly home, Goose." Morgan turned to face him. She was not in the mood to deal with him when her anxiety was already through the roof. "You have successfully delivered me to my destination."

"A gas station?" He asked, looking around.

The click of the pump caught her attention. She quickly put everything away before moving toward Goose. She was not going to bring a stranger to see Sally. Only one person in Maple Grove even knew about

Morgan's past and she wanted to keep it that way. Sally was already upset about last night and there was no way on earth she was going to bring more drama to the table right now.

"I said you could be my wingman for an hour, Goose. That time is up. Now go back." Morgan stepped toward him.

"No offense, but I am more scared of Maverick than I am you. He is worried about your safety, and I will do my best to make sure you come to no harm." Goose crossed his arms over his chest.

Morgan reached up and grabbed his ear, yanking him down so that she could whisper in it. "I am not your responsibility." She growled before shoving him away. Morgan put her helmet on as she waited for him to head back the way they had come.

He rubbed his ear. "Feisty human girl." He muttered under his breath, but she still heard him. Goose shook his head and shrugged. "I am staying with you until you return to Maple Grove."

Human girl? Was Goose a werewolf? Morgan looked around the gas station. It was completely deserted except for the two of them. "I really am sorry." She whispered.

A look of confusion crossed Goose's face before she grabbed his helmet and swung it into his face as hard as she could. He stumbled back several steps before he fell against his bike. Both man and machine fell over. Morgan jumped on her bike and rode off as quickly as she could.

Morgan rode to the other side of the city, making sure to make frequent turns before heading back to the clinic. She parked at the back of the parking lot out of sight of the street before running inside. She felt so bad for what she had done to Goose.

Her guilt only intensified when she stepped into her sister's room. Sally sat on her bed with red and puffy eyes. Morgan climbed up onto the bed and held her sister. Sally clung to her tightly as Morgan rocked her gently.

* * *

Maverick's phone rang not long after they decided they needed to talk with Morgan about Jay. "Hello."

"Dude, your girl is something else." Charlie laughed through the line.

"What are you talking about? Is she okay?" Maverick asked. The others sat up straighter trying to listen. Maverick put the call on speaker.

"I finally caught up to her at a gas station. She told me that my hour of being her wingman was up and told me to go back." Charlie sniffed. "When I told her I would be staying with her until she returned to Maple Grove, she grabbed my helmet and hit me in the face with it. I think she broke my nose."

Maverick sat in stunned silence until Colt and Brett burst out laughing. "Where is she now?" Maverick asked.

"I have no idea. By the time I got to my feet, she was gone. That little human sure packs a punch." Charlie sounded impressed, but Maverick became tense.

His brother was missing and the only person who might be able to help them find him was his mate. And now she was missing too. He grabbed the bridge of his nose and squeezed his eyes closed. What had caused Morgan to run away? He knew he should have gone with her. He was desperate to make sure that she was okay.

"Just try to find her and keep her safe." Maverick finally said before ending the call.

Chapter 6

Sally finally stopped crying. Morgan leaned back and wiped the tears off her sister's cheeks. "I'm so sorry I didn't answer the phone." Morgan whispered.

"What happened? Why didn't you?" Sally leaned her head on Morgan's shoulder.

Morgan sighed. "We had a dog come in a few days ago. Some guys thought he was dangerous and tried to hurt him. Missy and I agreed that he needed to be hidden until we knew what to do with him." Morgan continued to tell Sally about the night of the attack.

"What does that have to do with last night?" Sally asked as she sat up and looked at Morgan.

"Do you remember the guy from the bar I told you about?"

"How could I forget the baby guy?" Sally smiled.

Morgan shook her head as she fought her own smile. "Well, Devon and Jake showed up at the shelter yesterday and demanded I give them the husky. The three of us went to the diner to talk about it. Wolf showed up as things began to escalate with Devon and Jake."

"What did Wolf do? Did he beat them up for hurting you?" Sally asked excitedly.

"No. He walked me back to the shelter where Missy told him about the other night with Devon and Jake. I don't know what happened. Memories from the crash and Luke hit me, and I broke down. Wolf held me until I was all cried out. I was so tired. I mentioned being afraid to drive home with how exhausted I was." Morgan shook her head.

"Tell me he drove you home and took care of you." Sally grinned.

Morgan laughed. "He took me to the hotel, gave me the key to his room, and told me to go rest while he went back to work."

Sally's eyes widened in surprise. "You slept with him?"

"No!" Morgan yelled as her cheeks heated. "Of course I didn't. I have no idea where he slept, but it was not with me. I fell asleep alone and woke alone."

"When do I get to meet him? He sounds amazing." Sally's voice took on a dreamy quality. "If you don't want him, can I have him?"

Morgan flicked her sister's forehead. "You are only fourteen, dear sister."

"Then you need to give him a chance." Sally fixed Morgan with a glare. "Promise me you won't drive him away."

Morgan studied Sally's face. She had the same golden blonde hair and brown eyes that Morgan had. People often mistook them for twins or for mother and daughter.

Morgan hated to disappoint Sally. "Okay. I will not drive him away and I will give him a chance."

"Thank you." Sally nodded firmly before a mischievous smile spread on her lips. "And I have your new theme song."

"No." Morgan covered her face with her hands. When Sally was five and Morgan was fourteen, they started assigning theme songs to one another, and the person would have to sing along with the song whenever it played.

"'Meant To Be' by Bebe Rexha." Sally clapped in excitement. "Now what are we doing this weekend?"

Morgan laughed as she climbed off the bed. She peeked in the hallway to make sure no one was there and moved back to Sally. Morgan gave Sally a piggyback ride out to her bike. She handed her sister the helmet before they rode to a park on the outskirts of town.

They picked up fast food for a picnic lunch along the way. After lunch, Morgan used her phone to play music as they lay in the grass and watched the clouds lazily cross the sky. They laughed and sang while soaking up the sun for hours.

The sun was starting to set when a shadow crossed over Morgan seconds before a large figure stood over them. Sally screamed and Morgan jumped to her feet, ready to defend them at all costs. The man was huge, and Morgan's heart raced in fear. She let out a sigh when she recognized Goose. He stood with his stance wide, arms crossed over his chest and narrowed eyes. He did not look happy.

Morgan swallowed nervously as she moved her body in front of Sally. "I didn't expect to see you for a few days." Morgan finally broke the silence.

"You mean because you slammed my helmet into my face? Did you think I would head back home with my tail tucked between my legs?" Goose raised an eyebrow. "Your safety comes first."

"You hit this guy in the face with a helmet? Morgan, he is huge." Sally's anxious voice asked from the ground behind Morgan.

Goose's eyes dropped to Sally and blinked in surprise as if he hadn't noticed her there yet. "Eyes up here, Goose." Morgan said in a tight voice. When he looked at her, he cocked his head as if trying to puzzle something out.

"You were upset when you left. We were worried. Especially since you are still sporting that swelling on your cheek." Goose looked between Sally and Morgan.

"Morgan, who is this guy?" Sally whispered.

"I honestly don't know. He is friends with Wolf. But that's all I know." Morgan looked at Goose in disbelief. "Why are you even here? I am no one to you."

"You are important to Maverick, which makes you important to me. It's that simple." Goose shrugged before taking a seat on the grass. He was several feet away from them, but Morgan still didn't feel fully comfortable with him there. "And my name is Charlie."

Morgan slowly sat as well. Sally wrapped her arms around Morgan's arm. Morgan could feel her shaking. "You do realize that I don't even know Maverick either, right?" Morgan asked as she pulled her arm from her sister's grasp and wrapped it around her in a hug.

"Whose Maverick?" Sally asked and then sat up straight and looked at Morgan with wide eyes. "Wait!"

"Yes." Morgan sighed in answer to her sister's unasked question.

Sally looked between Goose and Morgan several times before bursting out laughing. "And this is Goose?"

"Yup." Morgan's lips twitched.

"And his name really is Maverick?"

"It appears so." Morgan tried to resist the urge to laugh along with her sister but failed. She knew her sister would find it hilarious.

"Now you really have to. Its destiny." Sally said as she laughed.

It took several minutes for them to get control over themselves. They were both lying on their backs, heads close together with large smiles on their faces. Sally turned her face so she could see Morgan.

"When can I come home?" Sally asked. The mood immediately sobered.

Morgan rolled on her side. She tucked Sally's long hair behind her ear. "I will talk with the doctor tomorrow, Love." A lump formed in her throat. She wished she could take her home this weekend, but the odds of that were slim to none. "Shall we head back and smuggle in some burgers?"

Sally blinked rapidly before sitting up. Morgan sat up as well and nearly screamed when she saw Goose sitting close by watching them. She had forgotten he was there. She swallowed before picking up her phone and turning the music off. Sally climbed on her back, and they headed back to her bike.

Goose followed behind them through the drive thru and back to the clinic. As they approached the front doors, they opened. Dr. Harvey held it open for them with an angry scowl. Morgan's steps never faltered as she walked past him. She heard Dr. Harvey telling Goose that visiting hours were over, and he would have to come back in the morning.

Morgan continued on to the room and set Sally down on her bed. Dr. Harvey came storming in not long after. "What were you young ladies thinking?"

"We only went to a park and were watching the clouds." Morgan shot back.

"On a motorcycle with only one helmet? Ms. Elliot, that was dangerous." Dr. Harvey paced the small room with his hands behind his back. Morgan's heart began to pick up speed as she listened to the lecture. This one was different from all the others he had given her. "I have looked the other way every time you two have snuck out, but I can't anymore. In two weeks, it will be the last time you will be allowed to visit your sister here."

"What? You can't do that." Morgan's hackles rose. No one was going to keep her from Sally.

"I can." Dr. Harvey turned to face them fully. "Because we are releasing Miss Sally two weeks from today."

Morgan stood in shocked silence until Sally squealed. Dr. Harvey's stern expression melted into a smile before nodding and walking out the door. Morgan embraced her sister as they both cried and laughed.

* * *

Morgan rode up the long driveway to the cabin. She had managed to ditch Charlie. After Sally had gone to bed that first night, Morgan went outside to get some fresh air. She wasn't surprised to find Goose there. She explained about the accident and Sally's recovery. She purposely left out all talk of Luke. Just focusing on the fact that they were rolled in a car and both of them were injured because of it. She made him promise to keep the accident and Sally a secret before going back inside.

Over the weekend, Goose and Morgan talked more. She found out he was a pretty cool guy. Even though he was the size of a giant, Goose was super sweet and kind, which only made her feel guilty about lying to him.

She had told him she would meet him at the gas station so they could top off before heading back to Maple Grove. She was surprised he left, considering she had filled up on the way in. She told him that she needed to speak with Dr. Harvey and would meet him there in a few minutes. As soon as he left, Morgan headed in the opposite direction. It added an extra two hours to her drive, but she didn't have to go through Maple Grove to get home.

The cabin came into view and Morgan smiled. In two weeks, Sally would be coming home with her. Taz greeted her with exuberance as she walked in the door. She laughed and gave him a hug.

"I missed you too, Taz." Morgan patted his head. She spotted a piece of paper on the counter. "What's this?" she asked as she picked it up. Taz barked.

The note was written in chicken scratch. Morgan read it quickly and sighed. Eli really needed to back off. This wasn't his house. He had no business just walking into her home. She looked down at Taz. He also had asked where she had been.

"I had a bit of a complication Thursday at work and slept at the hotel instead of coming home. On the weekends I drive to Jeffersonville, and I didn't think to call. I'm sorry. I'm not used to someone else being here. Just leave a list of what you need to replace all the locks on the doors and what security cameras you want me to get. I will get them before coming home tomorrow." Morgan moved to the fridge and pulled out the jelly. "Peanut butter and jelly sound good?"

They ate while watching several movies. Taz howled and barked at her when she put on Pride and Prejudice, but he watched it anyway. Morgan went to bed just after midnight and fell asleep quickly.

Morgan woke up drenched in sweat again and breathing hard. She wiped the tears off her cheeks and curled into a tight ball. Why could she not get rid of these stupid dreams?

Morgan got up and went into the kitchen. She made brownies and cupcakes to fill the time until she needed to leave for work. She packaged the treats and wrote two quick notes. Morgan grabbed the list of supplies Taz had written down during the night and jumped in her truck.

She made it to town just before six o'clock and walked into the hotel. She approached the desk with a big smile. "Good morning."

"Morning, ma'am. What can I do for you?" The desk clerk asked.

"I need this to be delivered to room 411." Morgan handed the box over to him and he nodded. "Thank you."

Morgan's next stop was the shelter. She was greeted with howls and barks. She smiled as she got to work cleaning kennels and exercising the dogs. She left a brief note for Missy letting her know that she took several of the dogs to the field.

* * *

Maverick was still irritated that Charlie had lost Morgan again. He could not believe that this girl could be so hard to keep track of. She was driving him insane. After that one night with her, he couldn't seem to sleep. Timber kept whining about wanting to hold his mate. Maverick couldn't deny that he was desperate to see her again as well.

A knock sounded at the door and Colt answered it. When he walked back to the sitting area, he was holding a box. "It's for Goose." Colt said confused.

"Goose? Let me see." Charlie took the box from Colt. He set it on the table before lifting an envelope off the top of it. Maverick watched as Charlie quickly read the note inside. Charlie started laughing and opened the box.

"What did it say?" Hank asked. "Who is it from?"

"It says: Sorry for breaking your nose. Maybe next time you will learn when a girl says to leave, you should probably leave. Just in case you don't, have one on me. Wingwoman." Brett read the note out loud.

Charlie started laughing even harder as he pulled out several instant ice packs from the box. "She even made enough brownies and cupcakes for everyone." Charlie looked up with a smile. "There is another note here."

Charlie pulled out a folded piece of paper and handed it to Maverick. 'Wolf' was written across the front. He unfolded the paper and read. He shook his head and tossed the paper to the side.

"What did she say?" Bentley asked.

"That I need to not send stalkers to follow her unless they are up for the challenge and that she wants her sock back." Maverick smiled. "At least we know she is back in town."

* * *

Morgan finished her obedience training with the dogs. She decided to let them run for a bit before heading back to their kennels. She sat in the large field with her phone playing music. Diesel and Jasmine were chasing each other around the baseball field sized clearing while Timon and Pumba laid beside her in the cool grass. It was a gorgeous day. The sun was shining, the dogs were playing, and Sally was coming home soon.

Morgan laid back and closed her eyes allowing the sun to warm her face. Her thoughts turned to Maverick. It was crazy that she had only known him for a few days, but she missed him. With some of Charlie's comments, she suspected that they were both werewolves. The question was, why are they hanging around a place like Maple Grove?

She was just starting to doze when Diesel's play barks turned aggressive. Morgan threw her hands over her face and groaned. "If you are here to ask about the husky, the answer is no!" She sat up and turned to face the gate, fully expecting to see Jake, Devon, or Eli.

Maverick stood there watching her with a smirk. "Can I come in?" he asked over Diesel's barking.

Morgan got to her feet and called for Diesel. The Doberman hesitated for several seconds, then ran back to Morgan's side. She grabbed his collar as Maverick stepped into the enclosure. He kept his movements slow as he approached. His eyes never left Morgan's.

When he was close enough, Maverick knelt on the ground and angled his body away from Diesel. Diesel continued to bark for several minutes, but Maverick remained calm. Morgan let out a tense breath when Diesel sniffed Maverick, and then he calmed down. She let go of his collar and he ran off after Jasmine.

"He seems like a handful." Maverick commented as he moved into a sitting position with his hands braced behind him.

"He is. We found him last month tied to a tree a few miles outside of town. He is fine with everyone but men." Morgan said as she sat back down in the grass.

They lapsed into silence as they watched the dogs on the far side of the field. "Charlie is the farthest thing from a stalker." Maverick said. "Especially since you agreed to have him go with you."

Morgan looked over at him as she smiled. "I agreed to an hour. He wouldn't leave."

"He may not have been a stalker before, but you might have made him into one now." Maverick chuckled. "You impressed him by fighting back and managing to slip away from him, twice."

"Okay, I feel terrible about hitting him and leaving him there. The second time was necessary to prevent him from finding out where I live." Morgan leaned back on her hands and turned her face to the sun. "I don't want a lot of people knowing my address."

"Why's that?"

"I have had enough of people to last me a lifetime." Morgan sighed. "I'm tired of it all. Get better soon, he wanted me not you, when can we drop by cards, you are unfit for the responsibility." Morgan shook her head. "I just want to forget."

When there was no response for several minutes, Morgan glanced over. Maverick was watching her with a puzzled expression. He didn't ask, even though she could see the questions in his eyes. He scooted a little closer and her heart picked up speed.

Maverick cocked his head to the side before a teasing smile appeared on his lips. "Baby, do I make you nervous?"

Morgan tried to keep calm, but when he moved close enough that his shoulder was touching hers, Morgan's heart kicked into overdrive. Maverick's smile grew. "You know its rude to do that." Morgan said as firmly as she could.

Maverick laughed. "It's kind of hard not to when it's beating so loud. If you want, I can slow it down for you."

Morgan swallowed hard and looked into his eyes. "And how are you going to do that?" Morgan asked. Maverick slowly slid his hand to the back of her neck and leaned forward. "Maverick, I can't." Morgan whispered.

"Trust me." Maverick's voice was barely above a whisper.

Instead of kissing her like she thought he was going to, Maverick rested his forehead against hers. Morgan drew in a shaky breath as she reminded herself to enjoy the moment and to give him a chance. She concentrated on breathing slowly. His unique scent filled her lungs, and she closed her eyes.

After a few breaths, Morgan found herself relaxing. There was something about Maverick that was calming. She sighed and Maverick leaned back. Morgan slowly opened her eyes to see him with a tender smile on his lips as he watched her.

"Better?" Maverick asked softly as his thumb brushed her cheek.

"Strangely, yes." Morgan smiled and sat further back. Maverick winked at her, which caused her cheeks to heat. She frantically searched her mind for something to say, anything to get him to stop looking at her like that. "If you are going to stay and hang out, you need to sit back and relax." Morgan reached for her phone and turned up the music.

"Is that so?" Maverick chuckled. "I could use a good relaxing day with you."

Morgan ignored the comment as she leaned back on her elbows and closed her eyes. They listened to several songs before her new theme song came on and she sat up quickly. She closed her eyes and shook her head as she silently cursed her sister and this stupid theme song game they played.

She kept her eyes closed, allowing herself to get lost in the music. "I don't mean to be so uptight. But my heart's been hurt a couple times by a couple guys that didn't treat me right. I ain't gonna lie, ain't gonna lie."

Morgan felt eyes on her, and she looked over at Maverick as she continued to sing. The corner of his lips turned up in a lopsided grin as he watched her. When the song finally ended, Morgan laid on her back and covered her face with her hands. Of course, that song had to come on while she was with Maverick.

"There seems to be a story with that song." Maverick's voice held a hint of curiosity. Morgan nodded but didn't look at him. "Can I hear it?"

Morgan sighed and turned her head to look at him. "It was assigned to me, so now I have to sing it whenever it comes on."

"Why was it assigned to you?" Maverick asked as he cocked his head at her as if trying to figure her out.

"Because, apparently, it is my theme song." Morgan covered her face again.

Maverick gently pulled her hands off her face. "Baby, whoever it was that hurt you was a fool. And if you have lost your faith in love, I would be more than happy to help you regain it."

Morgan's breath caught in her lungs. He looked so sincere, which frightened her. She fought the urge to get up and run away. Morgan closed her eyes. She reminded herself that it had been six months since Luke. She needed to start trying to trust again.

"I don't know if I can, Maverick." A tear leaked out the corner of her eye. Maverick brushed the tear away and Morgan looked at him.

"We can go as slow as you need, Baby. I'm not going anywhere." Maverick's voice was soft and full of determination. Morgan found herself slowly nodding, even though she wasn't sure she was ready to tear down the walls she had constructed after learning the truth about Luke.

She sat up and Maverick scooted closer to her before wrapping his arm around her waist. He pressed a kiss to her temple and Morgan leaned her head on his shoulder. A calmness settled over her and she closed her eyes. Morgan felt herself relaxing as her sleepless night started to catch up to her.

Chapter 7

Morgan settled heavier against Maverick. Her breathing deepened and he was sure she had fallen asleep. Maverick didn't know how she could while sitting up, but she had. He pressed a kiss to her head before slowly laying back on the grass. After what she had said about the song and being hurt before, he was sure that she was feeling a small amount of the mate bond in order for her to feel comfortable enough with him to fall asleep.

She cuddled close to his side as she adjusted her head on his shoulder. Her hand fisted his shirt before relaxing slightly. She let out a long sigh before falling into a deeper sleep. Maverick closed his eyes. This is what he had needed, to hold Morgan again.

What guy would be dumb enough to ruin things with her? He would do anything to keep her in his life. Sure, he had the mate bond pulling him to her, but he also liked her as a person. She was kind and patient. She was fiercely loyal and would fight for those she cared for. He loved her flirty and fiery sides. Whoever hurt her was most definitely a fool.

An hour passed and Morgan showed no signs of waking anytime soon. He wasn't sure when she needed to get back to the shelter or if the dogs needed water. He debated if he should wake her or let her sleep more.

"We should let her sleep." Timber said firmly.

"Are you saying that because you just want to keep her close?" Maverick asked.

"Maybe, but she also seems tired." Timber huffed. *"She is our mate. It is our job to protect and cherish her."*

"I am aware Morgan is our mate. But you heard her, she has been burned before. We need to tread carefully." Maverick looked down at Morgan.

Maverick ran his hand through Morgan's waist long hair. "Hey, Baby. Time to wake up." he said softly. Morgan groaned as she buried her face in his chest. "Come on, Babe. You've been asleep for an hour. We should probably start heading back."

Morgan looked up at him with a scowl, and he smiled. She shook her head and buried her face in his chest. He pressed a kiss to the top of her head. He couldn't help it; she was cute when waking up. She slowly sat up and looked around as she rubbed the sleep from her eyes.

Maverick stood and reached down to help her. He noticed that she would no longer look him in the eye. She accepted his help but took a step back as soon as she was standing. She was suddenly really tense, and her eyes were guarded when she finally looked at him. Maverick's stomach knotted with the look on her face.

"I need to clarify something." Morgan said as she wrapped her arms around her middle. Maverick's expression became guarded, and she felt a pang in her heart. "I don't know if I am ready for a relationship right now."

Maverick's jaw tightened, but he nodded his head. "I understand."

"No, you don't." Morgan shook her head. "Maverick, I have been…" Morgan's hands started to shake. She had never told anyone this about her, and she wasn't sure she was ready too. "I just need you to be patient with me." Maverick's eyes flashed to a deeper blue for a brief second. "You can tell your wolf that what I need right now is friendship."

Maverick's stunned expression nearly made her laugh. He ran his hand through his hair, messing it up. Morgan bit her lip trying to keep the smile from her face. He was cute when he was rattled.

"My wolf?" he finally asked, his voice sounded tense.

"I'm not an idiot, Maverick, so don't treat me like one." Morgan bent down and grabbed her phone and the leashes.

She let out a loud whistle and all four dogs came running. Maverick still hadn't said anything by the time she was done hooking the dogs up. She grew frustrated the longer he was quiet. Did he really try to convince her that he wasn't a werewolf, even though she had already called him out on it? Did he really think he could keep such a thing a secret while trying to have a relationship with her? She was almost at the gate when Maverick grabbed her arm, pulling her to a stop.

"I don't think you are an idiot." he said firmly. Morgan lifted her eyebrow in challenge and Maverick let out a tense breath. The muscle in his jaw flexed several times.

Morgan pulled her arm away from him. "When you are ready to have an honest conversation, come find me." Morgan walked away and loaded the dogs into her truck. She didn't even look at Maverick as she drove away. Her heart felt like it was breaking a little with each mile travelled.

She didn't understand why she was close to tears or why she felt so betrayed by his attempt to lie to her. She took several deep breaths before unloading the dogs. She asked Missy to turn everyone away that was looking for her. Missy gave her a questioning look but agreed.

Maverick came to the shelter a few hours after Morgan returned. Missy told him that she was busy and couldn't talk at the moment. Morgan was hurt that Maverick would try to hide the fact that he was a werewolf from her when she already knew he was. She would not stand for lies.

The shelter closed and Morgan ran to the hardware store to get the supplies Taz needed. She was still upset about her conversation with Maverick and not really paying attention to her surroundings. She bumped into someone as she was pushing her cart around a corner.

"I'm so sorry." Morgan said quickly as she looked up. Charlie stood there with a smile. Beside him stood two men. One was tall with white-blonde hair and brown eyes. Morgan dubbed him Iceman. The other had black hair and a boyish face. He was definitely Jester.

"Hey, Blondie." Charlie greeted her. "Thank you for the goodies." He scanned her cart and raised a brow. "What are you up to?"

"Just getting supplies." Morgan shrugged.

"Looks like you are having problems around your house." Iceman commented. "That is quite the security system you are assembling."

Morgan glanced at him. "Not any more than usual." Unfortunately, Eli had been a problem from the beginning.

"Then what are you guarding?" Iceman asked with a tone in his voice that instantly put Morgan on her guard. "We could come take it off your hands for you."

Hailey said that werewolves were territorial and rival packs would occasionally fight each other. Was Taz from a rival pack? Well, if they were, Morgan would make sure they didn't get to Taz.

Morgan leaned forward as if she were going to share a secret. "Careful, Iceman. I don't like to be messed with."

"Brett was just teasing." Charlie smacked his friend on the shoulder, giving him a warning look.

"Keep a leash on your dog, Goose, or I will have to muzzle him." Morgan said quietly with as much steel as she could put in her voice.

She pushed past them and walked to the counter. She was aware that they were watching her as she got into her truck. Morgan turned to see them standing next to a jeep. She flipped them off before driving back to the shelter. She would be spending the night there just in case they tried to follow her.

Morgan locked the door behind her before pulling her phone out. She dialed her home phone and waited. "Hello?" a male voice answered, surprising Morgan. She hadn't expected anyone to answer. "Hello?"

"Hi, it's Morgan." Morgan said quickly.

"Hey, when are you getting back? I have all the movies lined up, so we don't have to watch any of that girly stuff you pick."

"Taz?" Morgan asked, still shocked.

He laughed. "Yes. You didn't think I stayed as a wolf the whole time you were gone, did you?"

"Well, no, but its weird hearing your voice." Morgan shook her head as she walked into the office and sat on the small couch. "How old are you?"

"You could ask me anything and your first question is how old I am?" Taz laughed. "I'm sixteen." He went quiet for a few minutes. "I want to thank you for saving me last week. You got hurt protecting me and I owe my life to you."

"You are welcome, and you don't owe me anything, Taz. Werewolves are just like humans and deserve to be treated with the same courtesies. I honestly cannot believe what kind of violence is allowed around here." Morgan closed her eyes as she rubbed her temple.

"Yeah, too bad not all humans are like you." Taz commented. "So what time are you getting back? It's not like you to be out so late."

"I picked up the things on your list, but while at the store, I ran into a little problem. I don't want them following me home, so I am going to sleep at the shelter tonight."

"You will be careful? I don't want you getting hurt anymore." Taz sounded worried.

"Don't worry, little brother. I will be just fine." Morgan laughed. "I'll come home early tomorrow evening."

"Little brother? I like the sound of that. Having an older sister as cool as you would be awesome."

They said goodnight and Morgan called Sally. They talked about all the progress Sally was making, but when Sally turned the conversation to Morgan, she groaned. Morgan told Sally everything that happened that day, including Maverick being a werewolf.

"I thought we might be able to make a go of it, but he treated me like an idiot and tried to lie to me."

"Yeah. But remember that he is in a very unfriendly town. Maybe he didn't know how you would react." Sally said softly.

"Then he shouldn't have tried to have a relationship with me. I would have found out eventually, Sally." Morgan shot back before taking a calming breath. "I just don't want to be taken as a fool like I was with Luke."

"It's still hard for me to see Luke in that light." Sally sighed.

"Well, his mistress just gave birth to his son, so I am leaning towards believing them." Morgan shook her head. "I'm going to go to bed and sleep this bad mood off. I love you."

"Love you too, Morgan. Talk to you tomorrow."

Morgan put her phone on the charger and turned out the lights. She was just starting to doze when one of the dogs started to howl and bark. She bolted upright and listened closer. Whining and more barking reached her. She turned on the lights as she rushed to the kennels.

Dexter, the Border Collie, was pacing and whining. Morgan grabbed a leash before making her way to him. He nearly knocked her over when she opened the door. After getting the leash on him, she walked him to the side door. She didn't know what had gotten into him. He was normally well behaved.

She opened the door but stopped before walking out. It was pouring down rain. A flash of lightning followed by the rumble of thunder sent Dexter into a panic. Morgan slammed the door closed and walked in the other direction.

"You wanna sleep with me tonight, boy? Storms can be so scary." Morgan asked as she glanced down at the dog. "Why don't we put on some music to help drown out the storm?"

Morgan kept the lobby light on as she walked into the office. She unhooked the leash and turned to the stereo system. She plugged her phone into it and turned on a mix. Dexter paced for a few minutes before settling on the couch next to her.

A loud banging at the front door caused Morgan's heart rate to accelerate as she got to her feet. She slowly peeked around the corner. A man's dark form was visible through the glass. Morgan grabbed the handgun in the desk drawer and cautiously approached the front door.

As she got close, the man looked up and Morgan scowled. Maverick stood there with his shoulders hunched against the storm. Morgan tucked the gun into the back of her pants. She tapped the closed sign as she glared at him.

"Come on. I just want to talk." He called through the door. Morgan studied him for a long moment. "Please." He begged.

Sighing, Morgan unlocked the door and walked to the supply closet a few feet away. She grabbed a towel and mop before turning back to Maverick. She leaned the mop against the wall and tossed the towel at him. He started drying his face and hair.

"That is for the floor." Morgan said as she headed back to the office.

A few minutes later, Maverick knocked on the door jam. "May I come in?"

"That depends on whether you are going to treat me like an idiot or not." Morgan stroked Dexter's soft head.

Maverick sighed and moved to sit on the desk chair. "You are not an idiot, and it was never my intention to make you feel that way." He ran his hand through his hair. "What gave me away?"

"Goose said a few things that made me think of something a friend had said to me several years ago, Diesel didn't try to kill you, and you could hear my heart beating." Morgan sat back and crossed her arms over her chest.

"You aren't scared of me?" Maverick asked.

"You are a person, Maverick. Just because you can also shift into a wolf doesn't make you instantly dangerous. There are plenty of humans in the world that are scarier than you." Morgan looked Maverick up and down.

He was completely soaked from the rain. His wet hair caused water droplets to run down his face and neck. He watched her closely as if trying to gauge if she was being honest or not.

"You said something about a friend." He said, his gaze sharpening on her.

"She was my best friend when I was growing up. She and her family weren't shy about sharing information about themselves." Morgan stated.

"Charlie, Brett, and Colt mentioned seeing you at the hardware store earlier." Maverick's voice was casual but there was a hint of something else in it.

"You can tell the Top Gun crew that my purchases are none of their business." Morgan narrowed her eyes.

Maverick ran his hand down his face and Morgan could see his exhaustion. "What am I going to do with you?" he muttered under his breath.

"You are going to say goodnight and go to bed." Morgan got to her feet and headed for the lobby.

"Morgan, wait." Maverick gently grabbed her arm, stopping her.

"You look exhausted. You should probably get some sleep." Morgan said.

"Where do we stand?" Maverick almost seemed desperate for the answer.

"In the lobby of the animal shelter." Morgan answered seriously.

Maverick tilted his head back and looked at the ceiling. Morgan couldn't help laughing. She wrapped her arms around his waist and gave him a hug. He returned the embrace, burying his face in her neck.

Morgan stepped back and gave him a smile. "We can start off as friends." At Maverick's disappointed look, Morgan's smile slipped from her face. "I am going to be honest with you and lay my cards on the table." she took a deep breath. "That song was accurate when it comes to me being hurt several times. It's not just me I have to think about, and I got burned pretty bad last time."

Maverick studied her face and nodded slowly. "Cards on the table. I am twenty-five, a werewolf, and live in a nearby pack. My wolf's name is Timber. And I don't want to be just friends, but if that is what you need right now, I am willing to be patient."

Morgan hugged Maverick again. She closed her eyes as he held her. "Thank you." She whispered. She felt him place a kiss on her head before stepping back.

"Goodnight, Morgan." Maverick gave her a small smile before ducking back out into the storm.

Morgan relocked the door and headed back to the office. She turned the music up and sat on the couch with Dexter. Her clothes were damp from hugging Maverick, and she shivered. She pulled the blanket over her and the collie before closing her eyes with a smile on her face.

Chapter 8

Maverick met Morgan at the field again and they spent a few hours talking while the dogs played. They talked about their childhoods, schooling, and some of their hobbies. Morgan admitted that her parents spent a lot of time drunk or gone. Even when they were there physically, they weren't really there. She had been the adult figure in her family since she was ten. Maverick told her about growing up in a pack and his two brothers.

He seemed less sure of himself, and it hurt Morgan to know that she was the cause of it. Morgan found herself wanting Maverick to hold her again, but he kept a respectable distance. He was doing what she asked and was trying to be her friend.

The rest of the week followed a similar pattern. Maverick would meet Morgan at the field, and they spent hours talking and getting to know each other. Morgan avoided talking about Luke, the accident, Sally, and what happened when she was sixteen. In the evenings she would go running with Taz and watch movies. While she was gone, he had finished the deck and set up the security system.

Maverick kept up the physical distance. Each night when she went home, she would be frustrated with him. He was great. He did nothing that would break his word in just being friends. But that was what was frustrating, and she didn't know why. For some reason she didn't want him to keep his distance. She wanted to feel his arms around her again, but at the same time, she didn't. She couldn't risk another relationship like her last one. Especially since she had known Maverick for such a short amount of time.

It was Monday and Morgan had spent the morning at the realtor's office signing papers and didn't get to see Maverick for their usual meet up.

She couldn't believe how much she missed him. Morgan had yet to see him after being gone all weekend with Sally, and she was desperate to be with him again. But the day was going to be a busy one.

Morgan spent the rest of the day helping organize and load up the dogs to be transported to the city. Each month the truck would come, and all adoptable animals were sent to the city where they had a higher chance of finding a home. Diesel was the only dog that stayed behind. He still needed a lot of work around men and wasn't ready to be adopted out.

"Can I take Diesel home with me tonight?" Morgan asked as she looked at the Doberman through his gate. "He shouldn't be alone."

"Sure." Missy smiled at her as she locked the back door. "Just bring him back with you in the morning."

Morgan excitedly grabbed a night's worth of food and Diesel before walking outside. She loaded him up in the truck. Before she could open her door. A hand slid around her waist. Diesel slammed against the window, snarling. Morgan whirled around only to come face to face with Eli.

"Hey, Doll." He murmured as he moved closer.

Morgan's heart was beating so fast she thought it might explode. She turned her head just as he tried to kiss her. His lips pressed against her cheek. It didn't seem to bother him that he missed her lips as he trailed kisses down her neck while she tried to shove him away.

"Get off me." Morgan hissed. Eli's grip on her only tightened. Panic started to settle in as he pressed her against the side of her truck, causing her head to smack the glass.

Morgan grabbed Eli's ear, yanking as hard as she could, causing him to cry out in pain. Morgan raised her knee and connected with his groin. He stumbled back in surprise. He looked up at her and she punched him as hard as she could in the face. He fell backwards, landing on the ground.

"Don't ever touch me again." Morgan shook out her hand.

"Morgan!" Maverick yelled as he ran down the street followed by Goose, Iceman, and Jester.

With a shaking hand, Morgan tried to wipe the feel of Eli kissing her off her cheek and neck. Maverick reached her and pulled her into a hug, and she started to cry. His arms tightened around her. "He...he..." Morgan tried to tell Maverick what happened, but she couldn't get the words out.

"I know, Baby." He kissed her temple and Morgan buried her face in his chest. "Charlie, call the Sheriff!"

Maverick continued to hold her. She could hear his rapidly beating heart as she rested her head on his chest. She blocked out what the others were saying and concentrated on his heartbeat.

Eli started yelling and Morgan shuddered. Memories of waking up in the pool house with only her shirt on and no idea how she got there, flooded her mind.

"Maverick." Morgan whispered squeezing her eyes closed. "I want to leave."

Maverick looked down at her and his arms tightened around her. "Charlie." There was a brief pause. "Morgan's not doing so well, I'm taking her to sit down. Keep that guy here and let the Sheriff know that we will be down the road."

"Got it."

"Baby, look at me." Maverick said in a soft but firm voice. Morgan opened her eyes. "Can you walk?"

"He didn't break my legs, Maverick." Morgan said quietly, which caused Maverick to smile a little.

"I'm more concerned about you passing out." He brushed the hair out of her face. "You don't have much color."

Morgan heard sirens in the distance and snuggled closer to Maverick. "Let's just sit in the bed of the truck." Morgan gasped when Maverick picked her up. Her arms went around his neck as he carried her to the back of her truck. He put the tailgate down and set her on it. "I could have walked." Morgan said as she looked into Maverick's eyes.

Maverick leaned close and lowered his voice so only she could hear him. "Timber didn't want to take the chance."

"Ms. Elliot." The Sheriff walked up to them. He gave Maverick a pointed look and gestured for him to wait over by the others. Maverick stepped away from her and Morgan clasped her hands together tightly to try to control her anxiety. "Those gentlemen over there say Eli Winters attacked you."

Morgan began to shake again. "Yes, sir."

"Tell me what happened." The Sheriff pulled out a notepad and pen. Morgan told him about getting ready to head home and him forcing himself on her.

Maverick, Goose, Jester, and Iceman stood near the sidewalk as they waited. Maverick's gaze never wavered from her. Morgan just wanted him to be next to her. The Sheriff patted her shoulder before walking to the patrol car where the deputy was watching over Eli.

As Maverick moved in her direction, Morgan's phone rang. "Hello." She answered as she pulled her knees to her chest.

"Where are you?" Taz's worried voice came over the line. Morgan closed her eyes.

"There was an incident, and I won't be home for a little while." Morgan just wanted to lay down. "I'll call you when I am heading home, okay?"

"You don't sound okay. Morgan, what happened?"

"I will tell you later. I've got to go." Morgan hung up and looked up at Maverick. She uncurled from hugging her knees and threw her arms around his neck. "You left me." Morgan said into his neck.

"I'm sorry, Baby. They wanted to talk to you alone." Maverick pulled her closer. "Believe me, I didn't want to let you go."

"Excuse me, Ms. Elliot." The deputy said. "I was asked to take photos for evidence since you wanted to press charges.

"Photos of what?" Charlie asked from beside them.

"The Sheriff said Ms. Elliot has marks on her neck." The deputy fiddled with the camera in his hands.

Maverick leaned back and tilted her face to the side. His jaw tightened as he looked at her. Morgan closed her eyes fighting the tears that wanted to fall.

"Okay." Morgan finally said as she stepped away from Maverick. "When you are done, can I go home?" Morgan asked in a tired voice.

"Yes, ma'am. We have your number if we have any more questions. The deputy took several pictures before walking away.

Morgan sighed as she closed the bed of her truck. She turned back to the guys. She studied them for a minute before shaking her head. There was no way she was in a state to drive all the way home. Morgan opened the front door and climbed in. Maverick stood in the open door.

"Missy took Diesel back inside." Maverick said as Morgan glanced into the back seat.

"Good." Morgan sighed and closed her eyes. "Can you drive me home?" Morgan asked without opening her eyes.

She heard the other doors of the truck open, and she knew the rest of the gang was coming too. Morgan pulled out her phone and dialed the house phone.

"Hey, I'm on my way back. I have some friends driving me. See you soon." She hung up the phone.

Morgan typed in the coordinates for the turn off and set it on the dash stand. She laid her head on Maverick's shoulder and let him drive. The car remained quiet, and Morgan began to doze.

"Hey Baby, I think you gave us the wrong location." Maverick's voice roused Morgan from sleep, and she sat up.

"Take that road." Morgan pointed to her driveway. Maverick glanced at her and followed her instructions.

"How are you feeling?" Goose asked.

Morgan swallowed hard and looked down at her hands. Goose leaned down to try to catch her eye. She shook her head and laid back against Maverick's shoulder. Maverick moved his arm and put it around her. The turn off meant they had another twenty minutes to the cabin, so Morgan closed her eyes again.

"I don't like this." Goose whispered.

"You don't like how remote Morgan lives or you don't like that a man tried to take advantage of her?" Iceman asked.

"Both." Goose muttered. "I can't believe we didn't teach that guy a lesson before we called the cops."

"My house isn't all that scary and Eli isn't worth it." Morgan sat up.

The conversation ended and Morgan wrung her hands. She didn't know what would happen when they got there. She prayed she wasn't making a mistake by having them drive her home. If she had been thinking, she would have just gotten a room at the hotel or stayed at the shelter again.

Morgan had just wanted to go home and take a shower. She felt so gross and violated. Just like after the party. What would have happened if she hadn't been able to get away from him? Her breathing started coming faster. The truck came to a stop and Maverick turned to face her.

"Open the door." Morgan said desperately. She needed air.

Goose jumped from the truck and Morgan was right behind him. She took in gasping breaths as the 'what ifs' started circling in her mind. She needed to get away. Morgan ran into the forest as fast as she could.

The road curved up ahead and would eventually end up at the house. It would take fifteen minutes to get there. She needed to get there now. She continued to run and came across a small path that she had blazed shortly after moving there.

She turned down it and pushed herself faster. The cabin came into view. She was almost to the porch when the door opened, and a teenage boy stood there. She slammed into him as she began to cry.

"Where's the truck?" Taz asked as he wrapped his arms around her.

"I-I need...to get...inside." She gasped out.

"What did you do to her?" Taz's voice was threatening.

"Me? I did nothing. What are you doing here?" Maverick's voice sounded angry.

Morgan turned to see Maverick with fire in his eyes. The truck skidded to a stop on the gravel driveway. Goose, Iceman, and Jester jumped out of the truck, but froze when they saw Taz standing in front of her protectively.

"How about we take this inside, please." Morgan was shaking and Maverick's eyes softened when they shifted to her.

Morgan ran inside and went straight to the kitchen. A shower would have to wait, but she needed to get the feel of Eli off her. She leaned over the sink and started scrubbing her neck as tears burned her eyes.

A hand settled on her back, and she glanced up. Maverick stood beside her holding a hand towel.

"It's not coming off." Morgan whimpered. "I can't get the feel of him off me."

Maverick turned the water off and dried her neck. He pressed a kiss to her forehead as he cupped her face. "Morgan."

"Maverick, please." Morgan closed her eyes. "I just want it to go away."

"What do you want me to do?" Maverick asked. He sounded just as tortured as Morgan felt.

"Burn it off." Morgan cried.

"Baby, I'm not burning your neck." Maverick whispered close to her ear. "Why don't we dance instead?"

"Dance? How is that going to help?" Morgan pulled back and looked up at him.

He put his hands on her hips as he started to sway. Morgan followed his lead. Maverick rested his forehead against hers, and she took in a shuttering breath. After a few minutes, Maverick pressed a light kiss to her cheek.

He continued to place light kisses along her jaw until he got to her ear. "You are safe, Morgan. No one will touch you without your permission." Maverick whispered. Morgan put her arms around Maverick's neck and let him pull her closer.

"I still want to burn it off." Morgan said.

He softly kissed her neck just below her ear. Morgan tilted her neck a little, giving him more access without thinking about it. He continued to press his lips to her skin as he moved slowly down her neck. She gasped when she felt his tongue slide along the spot where Eli had focused. Maverick stopped with his lips barely brushing her skin. Morgan's heart was hammering in her chest as she waited to see what he would do.

"Do you want me to stop?" he asked so quietly that she barely heard him. Morgan swallowed before shaking her head. "Good." His lips once again pressed to the spot she had been frantically scrubbing minutes ago. He alternated between kissing and sucking her skin and she bit her lip to keep from moaning. Morgan found herself getting lost in the sensation of Maverick holding and kissing her.

"Maverick." She whispered, her voice coming out airy. Morgan needed to stop him even though she didn't want him to. She only wanted friendship right now. She needed to remember that.

Maverick pulled back and looked at her. He could see regret in her eyes as she looked at him. She swallowed hard as her gaze dipped to his lips. She closed her eyes and gave her head a little shake. He rested his forehead against hers and waited. He knew she wanted to say more.

"I can't." her voice cracked as she whispered, her hand going into the hair at the back of his neck. Her other hand slid from around his neck and down his chest, stopping just over his heart. It was beating almost as fast as hers.

"As slow as you need, Baby." Maverick whispered back.

Morgan opened her eyes and looked at the man in front of her. She couldn't believe how incredibly patient he was. He very obviously wanted more than friendship but wasn't mad at her for needing time. That was more than she could say for Luke. He often got mad and yelled when she told him she needed more time. She pressed her lips to his scruffy cheek before laying her head on his shoulder.

"Thank you." She breathed out.

"Morgan, I don't want you looking in the mirror and reliving what that guy did to you." Maverick pressed a kiss to the top of her head.

Morgan furrowed her brow as she thought about what Maverick said but didn't understand what he meant. A shout from the other room caused her to jump. He stepped back and grabbed her hand. "Come on, I want to know how you and my brother ended up living together. Then we can talk about alternatives to burning yourself if you are still feeling that way."

Maverick led her into the living room. Taz stood by the fireplace with his arms folded over his chest. He looked so much like Maverick. If she had seen him earlier, she would have immediately known they were related. The others were standing on the other side of the room as they glared at Taz.

"What happened, Morgan?" Taz asked coming up to her. He turned her chin to the side and looked at her neck. It was probably red from all the scrubbing.

"Eli." Morgan said in way of explanation as she sat down and rubbed her temples.

"Do you even realize how worried everyone is, kid?" Iceman snapped. "You have been missing for two weeks."

"It wasn't my fault." Taz fired back. "I was hit by a car that was off-roading."

"You had a phone. You should have called." Jester scoffed.

"Were you ever planning on coming back or just letting your family think the worst." Goose added.

"That is enough." Morgan got to her feet and glared at Goose, Iceman, and Jester. "I am not in the mood to deal with you three right now. And you two," Morgan turned to Maverick and Taz. "I can't even right now." Morgan shook her head as she headed for her room. "Keep the yelling down and if there is going to be any bloodshed, take it outside."

Morgan slammed her door and locked it. She moved into her bathroom and got into a hot shower. She sank to the floor and cried as the warm water fell on her. Once the water got cold, she got out. As she was brushing her hair, Morgan chanced a look at her neck. She was sure that Eli had given her a little hickey before she could get him off her.

Morgan's eyes widened when she saw the mark on her neck. It was darker and bigger than she thought it would be. Maverick's words about not wanting her to look in the mirror and see Eli came back to her. A small smile curved her lips as she gently touched the spot. No, she didn't think of Eli. Now she thought of Maverick holding her in the kitchen. She just wanted to get back to him, to feel his comforting presence. She quickly got dressed in pajama pants and a tank top.

When Morgan walked out, Jester and Iceman were playing chess on the coffee table while Goose read a book. None of them looked at her as she walked quietly behind them on her way to the kitchen. Maverick and Taz were cooking as they talked quietly. She silently slid into a chair and watched them.

"I know I should have called, but I was worried someone would come and get me. Morgan got beat up protecting me and I feel like I owe her. The two guys that ran me over have been harassing her and then that Eli guy thinks he owns her or something. He has even shown up here a few times.

Thankfully, Morgan was gone each time. I've heard her talking to someone she visits in the city about all of his advances. I just wanted to protect her like she did for me." Taz stirred something on the stove.

"Mom and Dad are really worried, Jayden. We kept getting snatches of your scent around Maple Grove. I caught it when I first saw her at the bar. It seemed to be strongest wherever Morgan was, so we started keeping tabs on her, hoping she would lead us to where you were hiding." Maverick rinsed a dirty dish in the sink.

Morgan felt sick. Is that why Maverick had showed an interest in her? She was just the key to finding his brother. Well, she was glad she could get Taz back to his family. Morgan quietly left the kitchen and went back to her room. The stab of betrayal she felt was worse than when she learned of Luke's.

She threw a change of clothes and some toiletries into her backpack and got dressed in her motorcycle gear before she climbed out the window. She didn't want to face Maverick. She couldn't. Especially after today's events. She had foolishly let her heart get involved with the wrong guy, again. She was so tired of being used.

Morgan walked her bike out of the garage and glanced back at the house. Taz stood at the kitchen sink. He looked up and their eyes met. His eyes widened and he gave her a confused look. Morgan blinked back tears as she put her helmet on. Taz quickly moved to the side, out of view of the window when she started her bike. She didn't waste any more time. She heard someone yell her name as she shot down the driveway.

Chapter 9

"Who's at the house?" Sally asked as she shook Morgan awake.

Morgan had been at the clinic for almost a week. She had arrived late the night she left and spilled every juicy detail to Sally, including the part in the kitchen with Maverick. Morgan felt hollow. She was just going through the motions for Sally's sake. Today Sally was going to be released, but Morgan didn't want to go home.

She was afraid that Maverick would be there. She missed him terribly, but at the same time, he had been using her. Morgan had no way of knowing if any of it was real or just him manipulating her.

"They are. At least when I left, they were there." Morgan mumbled as she pulled the blankets over her head.

"This is Morgan Elliot's secretary. You have royally screwed up and will not be permitted to speak with her at this time. May I take a message?" Sally said in a very proper tone, infusing in a terrible British accent.

Morgan sat up with wide eyes before covering her mouth to stifle her laugh. Sally stuck her tongue out at Morgan as she listened to the person on the other end of the phone.

"I see." Sally's silly face instantly turned to a frown. "You have a lot of balls saying that after using and manipulating Morgan to find Taz. If you had been honest with her and told her you were looking for your brother, then you might have had a chance."

Morgan moved to take the phone from Sally, but Sally moved out of reach. "Morgan isn't engaged. Luke died in a car accident six months ago. The same accident that nearly killed Morgan and me. Then at his funeral, she found out he had several side girls, one of which just had his baby. Next time do your research correctly." Sally ended the call and tossed the phone back on the bed.

Morgan stared at her sister in shock. "What did he say to get you so mad?"

"At first, he said he wanted to talk with you. Said you mean more to him than just finding his brother. That he never tried to manipulate you. Blah-blah-blah. Then he said you weren't exactly honest with him either. And said you were engaged. I cut him off and set him straight." Sally shrugged.

"Why don't you get changed, and I will hunt down Dr. Harvey to see if we can get released soon." Morgan smiled at her sister.

As soon as Sally went into the shower, Morgan grabbed her phone and dialed her house number. "Hello."

"Taz?" Morgan kept her voice low.

"Morgan! Why did you run off?" Taz practically yelled into the phone. "Where are you? Mav is beside himself and going crazy. I have never seen him like this."

"Everything hit me all at once and I couldn't stay." Morgan swallowed. "I need space, Taz. I need a favor. Can you look after the house?"

"What really happened that day?"

"Eli tried to force himself on me. I was able to get him to stop just as Maverick and the guys came. It wasn't that big of a deal." Morgan explained.

"Then what else happened to cause you to freak out like you did? It's not like you to go into such a panic." Taz asked, his voice lowered.

Morgan took a deep breath and slowly let it out. It was time she told someone. "I was sixteen and my family just moved. I was invited to a party, so I went to get to know my new classmates. I remember arriving at the party and drinking from the water bottle someone gave me. I have snatches of memory of me telling someone to stop and being kissed. Next thing I remember, I was waking up in a pool house half dressed."

"What?" Maverick and Taz yelled at the same time Sally asked from the doorway.

"Sal." Morgan breathed.

"That's why you did homeschool. Why you never dated. Why you are afraid to get too close to guys." Sally said as tears brimmed her eyes. "Why didn't you tell me?"

"Sally, you were only seven." Morgan said. "I didn't tell anyone. Dad would never have believed me and would have told me to get an abortion. Mom would have just gone along with Dad." Morgan wiped her cheeks. "I was scared, Sally. I was sixteen and pregnant and had no idea who to go to or what to do. I ended up having a miscarriage at eight weeks. I lost the baby, and no one needed to know."

"Where are you?" Maverick's voice came through the phone causing Morgan to jump.

Morgan cursed and ended the call. "Morgan, this is huge. You can't keep something like that bottled up." Sally crossed the room on her crutches. "Why don't we rent a car and go to the coast for a little while. You always found the ocean healing."

"Already planning on a vacation?" Dr. Harvey walked in with a smile.

Morgan forced her emotions into the back of her mind and returned his smile. They were discharged forty-five minutes later. While they waited, she reserved a rental on the beach and a rental car. Morgan loaded all of Sally's things in the trunk while Sally climbed in. She felt the need to hurry, Maverick and the gang would be showing up soon. Morgan wanted to be on the road before they did. In no time, they had music blaring and were headed for Maple Grove.

*   *   *

She hung up on them. Maverick stared at the phone in Jayden's hand as the feeling of desperation to get to Morgan intensified. He needed to get to her. Especially after those two confessions. Someone had hurt his girl, and she was left to deal with the aftermath for years on her own, and then Luke had cheated on her.

He understood better now why she had reservations about getting in a relationship. Now he needed to speak with her. He needed to make sure she knew that he never manipulated her. He was well and truly in love with her.

"What do you think we should do?" Hank asked.

"I have to find her." Maverick stated.

"She is probably with her sister." Charlie spoke up. "She is going to kill me for saying this, but Sally is in a special clinic for physical therapy. The accident crushed her leg and she had to learn how to walk again. She has been there for months but was going to get released soon."

"The girl on the phone said Morgan and her were in an accident." Maverick said as he began to pace.

"Morgan had some broken ribs, a broken arm, and had a large piece of metal that impaled her abdomen. Sally made a comment about Morgan nearly bleeding out before emergency responders arrived." Charlie informed the group. "From watching the two of them interact, they are incredibly close. It also sounded like Morgan helped raise Sally."

"Okay, Charlie and I will go to the rehab clinic to see if Morgan is there. Jayden, you need to go home and at least talk with Mom and Dad before coming back here. I want at least one person here at all times in case she calls back." Maverick said as he headed for the door.

Jayden followed him out. "What are you going to do when you find her?"

"I need to talk to her. I have to figure out how to make her understand that I wasn't using her." Maverick ran his hand through his hair as they walked to his motorcycle.

"She's your mate, isn't she?" Jayden asked, stopping a few feet away.

Maverick realized he didn't have his helmet. He didn't have time to go back and get it. He climbed on his motorcycle before looking at his brother. "Yeah, she is." Jayden stood on the porch and watched as Maverick and Charlie drove away.

Maverick couldn't seem to get to the clinic fast enough. It had taken them an hour to get there and when they arrived, they were informed that the Elliots had left ten minutes before they got there.

They had been so close. Maverick felt like punching something. The best the nurse could do regarding information was that the two women waited for a rental car to be dropped off, but she couldn't remember what company.

Disappointed, Maverick and Charlie walked back to where they had parked. "We should head back to Morgan's. She will come home eventually. Maybe the best thing you can do is give her a little space."

Maverick looked up at the clouds and let out a long, slow breath. "I don't want to lose her. I messed up by not being fully honest with her."

"Yeah, you screwed up. But I don't think it is too late to mend things between you guys. She may be human and the mate bond weaker for her, but she still feels it." Charlie patted Maverick on his back. "After that guy attacked her, she wanted you. She sought you out for comfort. Women don't usually do that unless they have feelings for the person."

"I hope you are right." Maverick started his bike and headed back to Morgan's cabin, praying she would be there when he got back.

Chapter 10

Morgan nearly honked at the two motorcycles that passed her in a no passing zone. They were going dangerously fast as they whipped around her rental car. Her stomach clenched as she recognized them.

"Those guys are going to get themselves killed." Sally yelled.

Morgan shook her head. As soon as they got to the animal shelter, she was going to call the house and rake them over the coals. What did they think they were doing driving like that?

Ten minutes later, Morgan pulled into the shelter's parking lot. She helped Sally with her crutches, and they went inside. "Missy?" Morgan called out when she didn't see her in the lobby or office.

"Back here, Morgan. I'm just getting Diesel ready to go." Missy called from the back room.

"Stay here, I'll be right back." Morgan told Sally before entering the kennels. "What can I do to help?" Morgan asked when she found Missy in the storage room.

"All that is left to do is put the food and Diesel in the car. I'm glad you are taking time for yourself." Missy smiled as she carried a large bag of dog food to the lobby. Morgan followed with Diesel.

"Oh my gosh! He is so cute." Sally gushed when she saw the Doberman. "Are you sure we can't adopt him?"

Morgan laughed and shook her head. "We will see how this trip goes."

Sally and Diesel were in the car getting settled. "Are you sure you want to take work with you? The point of a vacation is to get away from work." Missy asked.

"I love my job, and Diesel needs a lot of training still. I don't want to lose all of the progress we have made with him." Morgan gave Missy a hug. "I really appreciate you giving me the time off."

"You and your sister need some time together. Just let me know when you are ready to come back." Missy said before heading back inside.

Morgan pulled her phone from her pocket and walked several feet from the car before dialing the house phone. "Hello."

"You do realize that a double line means no passing, right?" Morgan said as soon as she heard Maverick's voice.

"Morgan?" Maverick breathed a sigh of relief, which only made her madder. He could have died driving like he had been.

"That was incredibly stupid. You had to be going at least ninety!" Morgan snapped.

"Baby, calm down."

"Don't tell me to calm down, Maverick!" Morgan yelled as she fought back tears. She was so mad at him for endangering his life. Flashes from the car accident and seeing Luke's dead body next to her nearly choked her. Losing Maverick the same way would kill her. "You could have died. You and Goose both. It was reckless and stupid."

"Wait. How did you know we were out driving?" Maverick asked.

"Because you passed me in a no passing zone going ninety when the speed limit was fifty!"

"Baby, where are you now?"

"Maverick," Morgan sighed. "I'm leaving town for a while. I have some things I need to work out."

"Can we talk before you go? Are you coming back to the house first?" Maverick sounded desperate.

Morgan's heart ached. All she wanted to do was see him. But he had used her, and she didn't know if she was strong enough to face him yet.

"We are just going to buy clothes once we get to where we are going." Morgan whispered.

"Morgan, let's go! We are burning daylight." Sally yelled from the car.

"I'll be there in a minute." Morgan called back.

"Tell flyboy that he is going to have to fly solo until he can make up for being a nitwit." Sally smiled before getting back in the car and closing the door.

"Baby, please. Wait until I get there." Maverick begged. "I know I messed up."

Morgan closed her eyes, holding back the tears. "Stop driving like you have a death wish. I couldn't…" She took a deep breath. "I can't…"

"I'll be careful." Maverick said quietly. "Where are you planning on going?"

Morgan laughed lightly "Sorry, Flyboy, that information is above your paygrade."

"Flyboy?" Maverick said with a chuckle. "Another nickname?"

"That is what Sally is calling you now." Morgan couldn't help the smile that spread on her face. A jeep pulled into the parking lot and Morgan looked over. "Oh great. I got to go."

Morgan hung up the phone as she watched the two men approach. Devon smirked as he stopped a few feet away. Morgan was not in the mood to deal with these clowns.

"Where is the beast, Morgan?" Jake asked with a condescending smile.

"I rehomed him to a nice family in Jeffersonville." Morgan shrugged. "I think he will be much happier there than he was with me."

Devon and Jake glanced at each other before turning back to her in shock. "Are you serious?" Devon asked.

"As the plague. Now if you will excuse me, I need to get going." Morgan walked back to the car and climbed in.

Devon and Jake were looking at her in disbelief. She started the car and pulled out of the parking lot. Sally and Morgan drove in silence for several miles before Sally turned on some music. The tension around Morgan began to fade.

*   *   *

The sun was shining, and the sand was warm under Morgan's bare feet. Sally sighed beside her as they laid on their towels. The sound of the surf brought peace to Morgan's soul.

They had been at the beach house for two weeks now, and Morgan had to admit, she had needed this. They spent most of the day lying on the beach and soaking up the sun. Morgan also worked a lot with Diesel. He had come a long way in just the past few weeks.

Morgan was still doing her online therapy sessions and with Sally's encouragement, started opening up about what had happened at the party. She was meeting with her counselor several times a week and talking about everything. She was finally starting to come to terms with what happened and it helped her learn how she could move forward.

Sally had insisted on turning off the phone and going off the grid while they were there. Morgan thought it a great plan at first, but that only lasted a few days. Her heart just wouldn't listen to her head. Maverick had used her to find Taz. Luke had used her and the other three women to get what he wanted. And Morgan didn't want to be in a relationship with someone who saw her as a means to an end.

Her heart on the other hand, longed to be near Maverick. She wanted to feel his arms around her again. She had never felt safer and more protected than when she was with him. His crooked grin, the corny lines he said when he was flirting, the way he set her heart racing, how calm he made her feel. She missed it all.

Morgan sighed and sat up. She pulled her knees up to her chest, wrapped her arms around her legs and rested her chin on her knees as she watched the waves roll in.

"That is it. The next guy that comes up to us and asks you on a date, you have to say 'yes'." Sally said in exasperation.

"What? No." Morgan glanced at her sister before turning back to look at the water.

"You are thinking about him again and you need a distraction." Sally glared at her. "You need to decide if you love him and are going to give him another chance or if you are going to move on. You can't keep going like this."

"Like what, Sally? I have been working with Diesel, spending time with you, doing therapy, shopping."

"And being depressed, and hardly eating, and thinking about Maverick constantly." Sally pointed out.

Morgan pulled her eyes away from the waves and looked at her sister. Sally watched her expectantly. "So, you want me to go out on a date because…?" Morgan asked.

"If you go out with a different guy and feel guilty or wish the guy were Maverick instead, then you will know that you need to give him a call. However, if you enjoy yourself and forget about him, then let him down easy and move on." Sally shrugged at Morgan's shocked expression. "I watched a lot of reality TV at the clinic."

Morgan laughed and shook her head. Sally was right, she needed to figure out if she wanted to give Maverick a second chance or if she needed to move on. "Okay, the next guy that asks for a date, I will accept."

They spent another two hours on the beach before heading back to the house. Sally wanted to rest for a while, so Morgan took Diesel down to the beach for a little training. The Doberman loved the water and chasing the seagulls.

Morgan was standing knee deep in the water as she threw the ball along the beach. She kept the throw light so Diesel could get it without yanking on the fifty-foot training leash. He came bounding back. He was almost to her when he started growling.

Morgan looked around and noticed a man walking out to her. She called Diesel, who ran to her. Morgan started distracting Diesel by issuing commands. The man stopped a few feet away.

"Good afternoon." The man smiled at her.

"Good afternoon." Morgan echoed as she grabbed hold of Diesel's collar.

"Hi, I'm Miles."

"Morgan."

"Nice to meet you, Morgan." Miles said, rubbing the back of his neck. "So, I was hoping that maybe you would like to go out to eat sometime. Or we could go get ice cream. Or something."

Morgan blinked in surprise. She had honestly never thought she would have to follow through with accepting a date. She glanced behind Miles to see a group of guys not far off. They were trying to not be obvious as they watched them.

Morgan turned her attention back to Miles. He was a little taller than she was with golden brown hair and warm brown eyes. Morgan noted his deep tan and large muscles. He looked like he spent a lot of time working out. Overall, he wasn't bad looking, but he was no Maverick.

I was just thinking about going to get some ice cream." Morgan said. Might as well get this over with.

Miles smiled, showing off a dimple. Morgan tightened her hold on Diesel as they followed Miles back to dry land. She moved to her things and pulled on her cover up dress, so she wasn't just in her bikini. She felt a pit forming in her stomach as she walked beside Miles.

Luckily, there was an ice cream stand just down the street. Diesel kept growling occasionally and Morgan would have to issue corrections. He had come a long way with not trying to attack every male in sight in the couple of months she had been working with him. This trip had been good for him. He had been able to experience many different environments. Diesel was starting to gain more confidence and in turn, was becoming less fearful.

"He doesn't seem too friendly." Miles commented.

"Diesel has been through a lot. I have been working with him for the past several months so that he can be put up for adoption." Morgan said as she patted Diesel's head.

"You are a dog trainer?"

"Something like that." Morgan glanced over at him. He was looking down at the ground as they walked. He seemed so uncomfortable. They walked in silence and Morgan wished that this wasn't so awkward. Why couldn't it be as easy to talk with this guy as it was to talk with Maverick?

The ice cream cart was a blessed sight when it came into view. Morgan ordered a small vanilla cone while Miles got a large Rocky Road. They ate in silence and Morgan wondered why he even asked her out if he wasn't going to talk.

She had just finished when Miles finally broke the awkward silence. "Who is he?"

"Who?" Morgan glanced over at him as they walked back to the beach.

"I may be dense when it comes to a lot of things, but even I can see you are nursing a broken heart. Plus, you have something on your neck that I am guessing he gave you." Miles chuckled. "So, either he left you and you are still pining after him, or you left him for doing something stupid, yet you still have feelings for him."

"It's not that simple." Morgan sighed as she sat in the sand. "I had a fiancé that died in a car accident. At his funeral, I met his three mistresses, one of which was pregnant with his child. Then I met another guy six months later. He said he wanted a relationship. I told him I could only offer friendship at the time, and if he wanted more, he needed to be patient with me. He said he wasn't going anywhere, and we could take things slow."

"Your beloved not only died but betrayed you. I get why you were not ready to trust again, but this new guy was willing to wait. He sounds like a decent person." Miles said softly. "So, what happened?"

"I found out that he was using me. He and his buddies thought I could help lead them to his brother, who had been missing for a few weeks." Morgan leaned back on her hands.

"Did you?" Miles asked. "Know where his brother was, I mean?"

"Yeah, I knew where he was. I had no idea the two were brothers or that he was looking for anyone. He never once asked me if I knew. He just kept tabs on me and hoped I would lead them there." Morgan huffed out a breath. "If he had just asked if I had seen his brother or if I knew where he was, I would have answered him truthfully. There didn't need to be all the secrets."

Miles let out a low whistle. "Wow." He looked over at Morgan. "Have you talked to him about it?"

"Not yet. I needed time to think things through before facing him again." Morgan looked up at the sky. "I had been used by my fiancé and I don't want to end up in that kind of relationship again."

"I get it. No one wants to be taken in twice like that." Miles said. "Has he said anything or tried to reach out now that he found his brother?"

"He says he knows he messed up and wants to talk."

Miles bumped her shoulder. "Can I give you some insight into the male brain that might be helpful?"

"Sure." Morgan looked over at him.

"Despite your best efforts, I would bet you have feelings for this guy and not the friendship kind." Miles smiled at her. "As for the guy's motives, it could have started out with him finding his brother, but he ended up falling for you. A guy would not put any effort into trying to fix something that he didn't want to work."

"So, you're saying I should forgive him?"

"I am saying you should talk to him. Maybe it is exactly how you thought it was. But if it isn't, you could end up regretting not talking with him." Miles got to his feet and smiled down at her. "Best of luck, Morgan. I hope your guy doesn't end up being a total dirtbag."

"Thanks for the advice, Miles." Morgan laughed.

She sat in the sand and thought about what Miles had said. He could be right. Maverick seemed desperate to talk with her before she left. What if he wasn't there when she got back? What if he decided to move on and that she wasn't worth it?

The sun was beginning to set, and Morgan was still looking out over the waves. Most of the beachgoers had left for the day. Sally plopped down next to Morgan, startling her. "I was wondering if you were ever going to come inside."

"Sorry, Sally. I was just thinking." Morgan said tiredly.

"I saw you sitting with some hottie earlier." Sally hedged.

"That was Miles. He asked me out for ice cream." Morgan smiled at the shocked look on Sally's face. "Then we talked about Maverick."

"You didn't." Sally breathed out.

"He asked about him and offered some advice from a male perspective. He said that a guy doesn't put in the effort unless he wants something to work." Morgan patted Diesel's side. "Should we go in and get dinner?"

They headed inside and ordered take out. Then they binge watched chick flicks before going to bed. Morgan lay awake all night thinking about what Miles said. She really needed to talk with Maverick. She needed answers that only he could give.

Morgan was eating a bowl of cereal when Sally emerged from her room. "Good morning sleepy head." Morgan said from the kitchen bar. "What do you want to do today?"

"Can we go to a spa?" Sally asked sitting down on the stool next to Morgan. "Like get massages, sit in hot tubs, get manis and pedis and get our hair done. The works."

Morgan laughed. "Why don't we do a few days at a spa to get everything done?"

"And can we go shopping? I don't have hardly any clothes." Sally asked excitedly.

"Let's spend a few days shopping, then a couple days at the spa followed by makeovers. Then we need to head home."

"Really?" Sally turned to face Morgan fully.

"Really, really." Morgan laughed as she got up and rinsed her bowl. "Eat so we can get the day started."

Chapter 11

Maverick slammed the phone down and ran his hand through his hair. Morgan's phone was now turned on, but she still didn't answer. It had been three weeks since he had last talked with her, and he was going crazy.

"Phone still off?" Jayden asked.

"No, it rang. She just didn't answer." Maverick looked at his brother. "What do I do? I know I screwed up. I know I should have just asked her about you, especially after she called me out on being a werewolf, but I just..."

"You what, Maverick? Did you think she would be mad?" Jayden asked. "Morgan isn't one to just blow up for no reason. I can see where she is coming from. That Luke guy had told her he loved her and asked her to marry him, all while he was sleeping with other women. It had to be a shock finding out while she was grieving his death."

"I know she has every right to think that I manipulated her. But I didn't. In truth, she was more of a distraction than anything." Maverick ran his hand down his face. "I need to find her. I need to tell her..." He trailed off and shook his head.

"I hope she forgives you." Jayden sat back and smirked. "If you screw this up and I lose my sister, I will kill you."

"Sister, huh?" Goose laughed. "When did you two adopt one another?"

"She adopted me the night she brought me here. It says so in the animal shelter records." Jayden laughed. "She knew I was a werewolf, even though I never shifted in front of her. She would talk to me like a human, make fun of me for eating out of a bowl and even forced me to watch chick-flicks.

She would ask if I wanted to and then say she couldn't understand dog, so she would take it as a yes." Jayden smiled.

"Sounds like you two had fun." Maverick grumbled.

"Oh, we did. We would go for hikes after she got off work, before she started working on fixing up the other bedroom. She always had music playing or a movie going. I think it helped with the nightmares."

"Nightmares?" Hank asked.

"Yeah, she got them most nights. She would wake up screaming. She told me she was reliving the accident. They were going out to celebrate her graduation when an SUV crossed the center line and hit them. I heard her screaming out for Sally or help." Jayden shook his head. "She made a firm rule that I was not allowed in her room, ever. It was hard listening to her. That's partly why I felt like I had to stay. She needed someone."

Maverick stood, walked to the window and looked down the road. "Maybe this time with her sister is what they both need in order to heal from what they went through." Charlie suggested. "I know you and Timber are desperate to find her, Maverick, but you need to be patient. Isn't that what she asked of you? Don't burn the bridge down because you rushed her."

The phone rang and Maverick's heart nearly jumped from his chest. Jayden picked it up quickly and answered it. He looked at Maverick with a small shake of his head before handing the phone to him.

"Hello?" Maverick said, trying to hide his disappointment.

"Son, we have another job for you guys." Maverick's father said.

"You know I am a little busy right now." Maverick returned his gaze to the window.

"It has been three weeks, Maverick. I know your mate is important, but I need you guys to go to Jeffersonville and install a security system for a new bank being built."

Maverick pinched the bridge of his nose. Maybe this job will take his mind off waiting for Morgan to get back. "When and how long?" Maverick asked.

"You need to leave first thing in the morning. The job should take two to three weeks." His father said.

"We will be home in a few hours to get everything ready." Maverick hung up the phone and looked over his shoulder. "We have a job in Jeffersonville tomorrow."

"What about Morgan?" Jayden asked, jumping to his feet. "Someone needs to be here when she gets back."

His father wanted the whole crew on this. But Morgan had asked that someone keep an eye on the house while she was away. He closed his eyes as he raked his mind for someone who could stay at the cabin for a few weeks.

He took his phone out and dialed his twin's number. "Hey Dallas, I need a favor."

"That depends on what kind of favor you are asking." Dallas chuckled. "If you are asking for advice on women, I am frequently in the doghouse, so I don't think I am the person you want to ask."

"No, man, I was hoping your wife might be up to a vacation. Dad is sending us to Jeffersonville for a few weeks, and I need someone to housesit while we are gone." Maverick said.

"Hey, Sweetheart. Do you want to go hang out at a cabin for a few weeks while we go on that job?" Dallas called out. There was a brief pause. "She says she is game."

"Tell her thanks for me. We will be back at the pack in a couple of hours."

"No problem. See you soon."

Maverick hung up and the guys cleaned up the dishes they were using for lunch. He hated having to leave, but he knew Charlie was right, he needed to have patience. Morgan deserved at least that from him.

*   *   *

Morgan pulled off the main road onto her driveway. She was both excited and anxious to get back to the house. She had no idea what Maverick would do when they saw each other again. Over the last week, Morgan came to the conclusion that she wanted to see how things went. If he truly was sorry, she was willing to give him a second chance.

"Is this it?" Sally asked, looking out the window. "It seems like the start of a scary movie where the two girls go to a remote cabin and end up getting murdered."

Morgan laughed. "It's not like that. Once we get to the cabin, you will see that it doesn't have that feel."

Sally turned down the music as they turned the last corner, and the cabin came into view. Morgan smiled when she saw the front door open. Her smile fell, the person that came out was not who she expected. Instead of one of the guys, a woman came out with her hands on her hips.

Morgan slowed down as they approached the front of the cabin. She slammed on the brakes when she finally recognized the woman. She threw the car into park and jumped out.

"Morgan Nicole Elliot, where have you been?"

Morgan rounded the front of the car just as her friend crashed into her. They were both crying as they hugged. "Hailey? What are you doing here? How are you here?"

Hailey pulled back and laughed. "Would you believe me if I told you we have a mutual friend."

"Hailey?" Sally asked as she got out of the car. "Is that you?"

"Hey, squirt. Long time no see." Hailey walked over to Sally and gave her a hug. "What happened to your leg? You know what, let's get the car unloaded and get you two inside, then we can catch up."

Hailey helped Morgan grab their bags and Diesel while Sally went inside. They unpacked while Morgan and Sally told Hailey about their beach trip. Once finished, they sat on the couch with glasses of lemonade.

"How did you end up here?" Morgan asked Hailey.

"That is a great question. Seems you ran off leaving two very disgruntled men to house sit for you." Hailey raised her brow.

"They were mad?" Morgan asked, looking down at her hands.

"I wouldn't say mad…more like upset. Jayden misses you and couldn't believe you didn't say good-bye. Maverick has been quiet and irritable." Hailey let out a laugh. "I had no idea that they were talking about you this whole time."

Morgan swallowed down her guilt. She did what she felt she needed to in order to work through her own issues. "What have you been up to since I last saw you?" Morgan changed the subject.

"I finished school. After graduation, I came to visit my Uncle Fred, he owns the bar in Maple Grove. While here, I met my mate, Dallas. He belongs to the nearby pack. We dated for a while and got married two years ago. He works at his family's business and is gone on a job right now with Maverick and Jayden."

"Mate?" Sally asked.

"It's a werewolf thing." Hailey waved her hand through the air as if it were nothing.

"What are mates? Is that what you call your husband?" Sally furrowed her brow.

"As a werewolf, we are blessed with a mate. A mate is someone who you are connected to on a deeper level. Almost like two sides of the same coin. We can recognize each other almost instantly. And once we do, we are drawn to each other by an invisible string. The chemistry between the two is insane."

"How so?" Morgan asked.

"Mates feel comfortable and protected when they are with each other. When they are separated, they feel almost desperate to get back to their mate. When they are together, they tend to always be touching in some way, holding hands, sitting close together, his hand on her back, hugging. If they choose to accept one another, they mark each other."

"Mark? Like a tattoo?" Sally's eyes were wide as she listened.

Hailey laughed and shook her head. "No, not a tattoo." She reached up and pulled the collar of her shirt down a little on the left side, exposing a silvery mark that had two distinct punctures and a unique design that connected them. "Our wolves push forward, and we bite into our mate's neck. Each mark is unique to the individual and lets other wolves know we are claimed."

"Doesn't that hurt?" Sally looked horrified.

"Yes and no. It hurts, but at the same time warmth spreads throughout your body. It only lasts for a few minutes and then it heals over.

As soon as the marking process is completed, we can feel some of our mate's emotions."

"That's so cool."

Hailey took a drink of her lemonade. "So, what have you two been up to?"

"Morgan was sexually assaulted at a party shortly after we moved. She took care of me like always and got engaged. We got in a really bad car crash where her fiancé died, we found out he was a cheating drug addict, and now we are here." Sally stretched her sore leg.

"Wait, what?" Hailey said in disbelief. "I think you need to start at the beginning."

"That is going to take a while." Morgan warned.

"Dallas isn't expected back for another week or two. We have time." Hailey pulled her feet up under her and got comfortable.

Morgan sighed and began with the move shortly after her parents discovered the Knights were werewolves. Morgan was only able to get to the part about finding out she was pregnant and how terrified she was. Then the miscarriage and the guilt she suffered for being relieved that she wouldn't be having a baby.

Hailey and Sally sat beside Morgan, and they cried together. They fell asleep on the couch and woke up late the next morning. Morgan showered quickly before she made pancakes for breakfast.

"You were always a great cook." Hailey commented after finishing her third plate.

Morgan laughed. "And you always ate a ton."

"Do you have to go into work today?" Sally asked.

"I should. I have been gone for four weeks." Morgan said as she rinsed her dishes.

"Sally and I can hang out while you go." Hailey offered. "Then we can meet you at Fred's Bar after work for drinks and dancing."

"I thought you said you were married." Sally pointed out. "And I'm only fourteen."

"Fred's is more of a hang out place with a dance floor and bar. You only need an I.D. if you are purchasing drinks. And I plan on only line dancing with my bestie and singing karaoke."

"You are still into karaoke?" Morgan groaned, but she couldn't help the smile that spread on her lips.

"You better believe I am." Hailey laughed. "We will meet you there at six and I fully expect you to participate."

Morgan was still smiling as she climbed into the rental car with Diesel. Having Hailey back in her life was a huge blessing. She hadn't realized how much she had missed her friend until yesterday. Spending the evening together had patched a hole in Morgan's heart she didn't know was there.

Morgan pulled into the animal shelter parking lot and walked inside. Missy screamed in delight when she saw Morgan. Diesel didn't seem happy to be back at the shelter and Morgan felt bad for him.

"So where did you go? You look fabulous, by the way. I can't get over how tan you are and how wavy your hair is now that it is short. You had to have cut more than twelve inches off." Missy gushed as they cleaned up dog poop from the side yard.

"Sally and I went up the coast and rented a beach house." Morgan said. "Diesel has been doing so much better. He loved the water. The three of us spent the majority of the trip soaking up the sun and enjoying the ocean."

"That sounds amazing." Missy sighed. "And how is your sister doing?"

"She is doing much better now that she is out of rehab. She still has to take things slow, but she is getting there." Morgan said as they moved into the kennel area and started cleaning out the kennels.

Missy went back to the office to do some paperwork while Morgan grabbed four of the new dogs and took them to the field. She turned on her music as she began working with a pit mix.

Lola was extremely energetic. Morgan started teaching her the different aspects of the agility course that they had set up on one side of the field. Lola took to each new obstacle quickly. When Tank, Buster, and Trike saw Lola running through the tunnel, they ended up following suit.

Morgan spent the next three hours working with each dog individually before taking them back. By the time all the dogs had been exercised, it was almost six. She quickly made her way down the road to Fred's.

Morgan's smile widened when she saw Sally and Hailey at a table near the back waving at her with such exuberance that Hailey nearly fell out of her seat. "What, are we teens again?" Morgan teased as she took her seat. Fred brought over bottled soda and complimented Morgan's new look.

"Uncle Fred, can we do karaoke tonight?" Hailey asked.

"I guess you can. We don't get much participation though." Fred said scratching his brow.

"You will tonight." Hailey clapped her hands as Morgan groaned.

They spent hours singing and laughing. Sally just kept shaking her head at Hailey and Morgan as they became more enthusiastic about the songs. Fred eventually came back over.

"If you ladies don't control yourselves, I am going to have to cut you off." He warned, even though he was laughing.

"You would cut us off of soda?" Hailey gasped in horror, which caused Morgan and Sally to start laughing.

"It's nearly one and I want to go home." Fred patted Hailey's shoulder with a laugh. "Come back tomorrow and we can put on some line dances."

Hailey squealed and hugged her uncle. Morgan followed Hailey and Sally back home. When they got there, they settled down on the couch and ate ice cream until Morgan called it a night and went to bed.

As she pulled the blanket up, Morgan noticed her bedding smelled different. She put it to her nose and breathed it in. Maverick's cologne? Had he been sleeping in her bed? Morgan smiled and she closed her eyes. For some reason the smell of him relaxed her and she fell asleep quickly.

Chapter 12

Morgan was on her way to Jeffersonville. She told Hailey that their line dancing party would have to be on another night. It had been a long day and Morgan just wanted to get home. But she needed to return the rental car today and pick up her motorcycle.

She was stopped at a red light when she glanced to her right. A man stood on a ladder outside a new construction. Her heart skipped a beat before double timing to catch up. He turned to face her as he talked to someone on the sidewalk. Morgan's heart sank. It wasn't Maverick. He looked so much like him it was crazy, but his hair was a little lighter and shorter.

Morgan turned her attention forward again. She needed to get a hold of herself. What would she have even done if it were him? Throw the car into park and run to him? No, she had to get to the dealership before they closed, and she couldn't stop traffic.

She let out a slow breath to calm herself as the light turned green and she drove away. Morgan made it to the dealership just before they closed. It felt good to be on her motorcycle again. She missed the freedom she felt when she rode it.

She put on her new motorcycle jacket. It was black with a deep purple design along the sides. She also got a matching helmet with a tinted visor. She smiled as she turned out onto the street. She pulled up next to a pickup truck pulling a trailer at a red light a few streets down.

"Hey, biker girl!" Someone yelled from the truck.

Morgan didn't even look over at them. The guy called again as the light turned green. She flipped them off and a chorus of laughter erupted from inside the cab. Morgan sped away and moved between several cars to put more distance between her and the truck. Probably not the safest way to drive, but she was tired and didn't have the patience to deal with neanderthals.

The cabin came into view and Morgan sighed in relief. It was almost nine o'clock and she was exhausted. After locking the garage, she started heading inside, but the squeak of the porch swing stopped her. Instead, Morgan walked around to the front and saw Hailey sitting there with a blanket.

"Hey." She smiled at Morgan. "You should join me."

"Where is Sally?" Morgan asked as she sat next to her. Hailey draped the blanket over both of them and handed Morgan a mug of hot chocolate.

"Her leg was bothering her a little, so she went to bed early." Hailey looked up to the stars. "Tell me about Luke."

Morgan choked on the hot liquid. "That was unexpected."

"It's just us now. Sally told me a little, but I want to know what really happened because I know you. You probably hid a lot from Sally."

Morgan sighed. "I met Luke two years ago. I was hesitant to be in a relationship because I was Sally's guardian, and it wasn't just me I needed to think about. But Luke was patient and kind. We went on a few dates before he asked me to move in with him. I turned him down gently. We dated for six months, and he was perfect.

"He bought gifts for not only me, but Sally too. Every Saturday we all played board games. He was supportive of both Sally and me. He attended her football games where she cheered. He even helped pick her up from different activities when I was in class or needed extra study time."

"He sounds like a great guy." Hailey said softly.

"I thought so."

"So, what happened? Why didn't you get married?"

"Every time we tried to set a date; I would panic. I just couldn't bring myself to. There were things about Luke that I wasn't the biggest fan of. I started having doubts. Luke grew frustrated with me after four months of us being engaged. After the party incident, I made a promise to never be intimate with a man until we were married. Luke thought I was being old fashioned. I only kissed him once when I agreed to marry him."

"He got mad that you were wanting to save yourself for marriage? That is crazy." Hailey set her mug down on the porch before putting her arms around Morgan.

"We started to argue more about it, and I had an even harder time wanting to set a date. We were engaged for a full year, Hailey. I felt broken because I couldn't seem to commit to him, even though I thought I was in love with him. Maybe I'm not meant to be with someone. Maybe I should adopt a dog and finish raising Sally."

"You are not broken, Morgan. From what Sally said, it is a blessing that you didn't actually marry the guy." Hailey squeezed Morgan and she closed her eyes. It was so nice having someone to talk to about this.

Morgan laid her head on Hailey's shoulder. "I graduated and we were heading out for pizza to celebrate. Luke was driving. We were rounding a bend in the road and a vehicle was coming straight for us. It was halfway in our lane. Luke laughed and asked if I could believe this guy. I screamed for Luke to do something. Then the car was rolling. I could hear Luke swearing and Sally screaming."

Hailey's arms tightened around her. "When the car came to a stop, I was in so much pain. Sally wouldn't respond when I called to her. I was stuck and could not move. Luke was mumbling about being sorry and wasting time, until he went quiet. I learned from EMS that Luke had died before they arrived. I was pinned in place by a piece of metal through my abdomen. I could see Luke, there was so much blood. I watched him die, Hailey."

"Oh, Morgan." Hailey sniffled. Morgan wiped her own cheeks.

"I was still not released from the hospital when Luke's funeral took place. A nurse was kind enough to take me. I was sitting in a wheelchair off to the side. I was still in shock and a lot of pain. Three women asked if they could speak with me. They told me they were Luke's girlfriends. One was six months pregnant, and another had a one-year-old on her hip. It turned out Luke wasn't into fully committing to someone."

Morgan sniffled and shook her head. "The night I got home from the hospital, two detectives came to my door. They asked about Luke's drug use. To my knowledge he never did anything like that. His autopsy showed that he was on something while he was driving. He also had a record I didn't know about because he gave me a false name. His real name was Lucas Garcia not Luke Grant. He had various drug charges. I was so stupid, Hailey."

Hailey sat up and grabbed Morgan's face with both hands. "You are not stupid." she said firmly. "You are an amazing person. Your instincts were telling you something was wrong with Luke, even though he put on a convincing performance."

Hailey held Morgan while her tears fell. She had desperately needed a friend during the past several years. Hailey whispered words of comfort while Morgan cried out all the hurt and fear from that time. When her tears were spent, they sat in silence and stared up at the stars until it got too cold.

* * *

"That motorcycle looks like Morgan's." Jayden commented as he looked out the window of the truck.

"The bike looks like hers, but the jacket and helmet are different. Not to mention that Morgan's hair would be hanging down to her waist and she is a lot whiter than that chick." Charlie said as he looked out the window.

"Only one way to find out." Colt smiled as he rolled down the back window.

"Don't be an idiot." Maverick shook his head. He had thought the same thing about the biker looking similar to Morgan.

"Hey, biker girl." Colt called out. The woman remained facing forward, but her body tensed. Maverick watched her out of the corner of his eye as he tapped his fingers on the steering wheel. "My, are you looking fine this evening." Colt tried again as the light turned green.

The woman turned slightly in their direction. Her visor was too tinted to see any of her face. She flipped them off and everyone started laughing. Maverick continued to watch her as she wove through several cars. He could imagine Morgan yelling at him again if she saw him driving like that.

A small smile spread on Maverick's face. Morgan had not been happy at all when she had seen him and Charlie riding fast. The guys had teased him, calling him a granny for driving slower. But he wasn't about to do anything that would upset Morgan if he could help it.

They got to their hotel and Maverick went straight to his room. He pulled his phone from his pocket and dialed the cabin's number. "Hello?" Hailey's voice answered.

"Hey, Hails." Maverick tried to sound like he wasn't disappointed to hear her. "How are things going?"

"Don't sound so down, Mav." Hailey laughed. "The answer is 'no' she hasn't called. But a bunch of furniture arrived the other day with instructions to put it in the spare room."

"How's the popcorn coming, Hailey?" A female voice called to her.

"Who was that?" Maverick asked. The voice sounded familiar, but it wasn't Morgan's.

"Just a friend. We are watching chick flicks tonight. And don't sound so surprised, I have friends other than the Storm brothers."

Maverick shook his head. "Don't ruin anything in that house."

"Don't worry, everything will be clean and ready for your return."

"Do you think she is coming home soon?" Maverick asked sitting up.

"Someone is planning on returning. There is a whole bedroom set and a porch swing." Hailey said brightly but there was something else in her tone. "I am a huge fan of the porch swing. I am going to ask Dallas to get one for our house."

"Keep me informed." Maverick sighed. "If she calls…"

"I know. I will let you know if she calls."

"Thanks, Hails."

"Try to relax, Maverick, all will work out." Hailey said sympathetically.

"I'll try."

Maverick hung up the phone and jumped in a quick shower before going to bed. He was going to push the crew hard tomorrow. They were going to get this job done as fast as possible so he could get back to the cabin. If Morgan was coming back soon, he wanted to be there.

*   *   *

Morgan spent the rest of the week busy with work. Missy got sick and Morgan had to enlist the help of both Hailey and Sally to keep the shelter running smoothly. By the end of each day, they were all too tired to do much more then go home and veg out on the couch.

Morgan was cleaning the kennels Friday afternoon when Hailey peeked her head around the corner. "Can I ask you something?"

"Sure." Morgan smiled as she scrubbed the floor of the last kennel.

"What exactly is your relationship with Maverick Storm?" Hailey asked, curiosity burning in her eyes. "He has called every day since he has been gone to ask about you." Morgan tensed. "Don't worry he usually asks if you have called, and I honestly tell him that you haven't."

Morgan kept her expression blank as she looked back down at the floor as she scrubbed. "What makes you think I have a relationship with him?"

"You asked him to watch your house, Morgan. Don't play dumb with me."

"I asked Taz to keep an eye on the house." Morgan said, turning back to her task. Hailey started tapping her toe. "Okay fine. Maverick said he wanted to help me regain my faith in love. I told him I didn't think I could. I wasn't sure I was ready for another relationship. I told him the best I could do was friendship."

"And…"

"And he said we could take things as slow as I needed because he wasn't going anywhere." Morgan scrubbed more vigorously. "We started hanging out more. When Eli got handsy, Maverick and the rest of the Top Gun crew came running. With Maverick there, I felt protected and safe. We were almost back to the cabin when memories of the party slammed into me, and I panicked. I ran from the car, desperate to get the feel of Eli's mouth off my neck."

Hailey took the scrub brush from Morgan and sat against the wall. "Then what happened?"

"Taz came outside and asked Maverick what he did to me. I got everyone inside and then tried to scrub my neck. Maverick came in and stopped me. I asked him to burn my neck to get the feeling to go away, but he refused. He said we should dance, and we started dancing. Just having him close somehow helped me calm down. I still felt violated and gross, but I wasn't frantic."

"Sounds like he cares for you." Hailey commented.

Morgan shrugged. "I took a shower and went to the kitchen to find Taz and Maverick cooking. Maverick was scolding Taz for not reaching out to his family, so they knew that he was safe. Maverick said that Taz's scent was strongest around me. They started keeping tabs on me, hoping I would lead them to him."

"He said that?" Hailey asked in disbelief.

Morgan nodded her head. "Did I overreact, Hailey? After I heard that, I was crushed. I felt used, just like I had been used by Luke. I couldn't stay there and face him. I didn't want to end up in another Luke type situation. So, I snuck out my window and left."

"Have you considered that there is more to Maverick's motives than what it appears?" Hailey asked, putting a hand on Morgan's knee.

"Yes. I've considered it. At this point, I need to talk with him to figure out what his motives were so I can decide what I need to do for mine and Sally's sakes." Morgan leaned her head back on the wall as she closed her eyes.

"You're in love with him, aren't you?" Hailey whispered.

Morgan turned her head to look over at Hailey. "Is it that obvious? I just barely came to that conclusion."

Hailey laughed. "Only because I might have insight that you don't. At least I think I do." Hailey rubbed her chin.

"What's that?" Morgan asked.

"Do you remember when I told you about meeting Dallas?"

"You said he was your mate."

"Humans can be mates as well. It's rare, and they can't have kids because of the whole hybrid thing, but it's possible."

Morgan turned to fully face Hailey as she furrowed her brows. "You think that I am..."

Hailey lowered her voice even more. "Maverick's mate. Think about it. You, who have had terrible experiences with guys and have developed a sort of phobia of them, feel comfortable around Maverick. You said it yourself that you feel safe and protected with him."

"I also felt comfortable around Taz." Morgan pointed out. "That doesn't mean anything."

"Sally told me about your melt down the day after meeting Maverick and how he held you before having you go to his hotel room." Hailey scooted closer. "Did you feel the least bit suspicious or threatened? I mean come on, Morgan, you went to a man's hotel room, and you didn't even know him."

Morgan blinked in surprise. She had. She didn't even think twice. Not once did she worry that Maverick would hurt her. She knew she was safe with him.

"Maverick has been calling the cabin at least twice a day since he left. I have never seen him even date, let alone desperate to see someone like he is with you. He is acting like he has lost his mate."

"If I am his mate, then why did he not say anything? Why did he use me like he did?" Morgan asked. "What does it even mean to be mates?"

Hailey grabbed Morgan's hand. "It means that you are the most important thing to him. Everything else pales in comparison. He will do everything in his power to protect and care for you. And the same goes the other way. He is the most important thing to you." Hailey smiled. "Home is wherever the other is."

Morgan chewed her bottom lip as she thought about it. She wasn't sure if what Hailey was saying was true. "How do I know if Maverick and I really are mates?"

"He could tell you. Or you two can go to an elder from the pack, and they can confirm it." Hailey shrugged.

"Even if we are mates, he used me." Morgan said.

"Oh, I'm not saying how Maverick handled things is okay. He was wrong and never should have used you like that. Make him work for it."

Morgan got to her feet and gave Hailey a hug. "I am so glad you are back in my life." Hailey laughed.

Morgan finished cleaning the kennels before taking the dogs outside for a little exercise. When she got back, Missy was chatting with Hailey and Sally at the reception desk.

"Thank you for taking over the shelter this week." Missy told them. "I think we can close now and get an early jump on the weekend."

"I am all for this plan." Hailey cheered. "We are going out tonight. No arguments."

"What are you ladies going to do?" Missy asked with a laugh.

"We are going to Fred's and spending the night dancing." Hailey declared.

"In that case, don't forget to go shopping for some new outfits." Missy shooed them out the door.

They drove all the way to Jeffersonville to go shopping. Morgan allowed Sally and Hailey to pick out a whole outfit for her, including boots and a hat. By the time they got back to Fred's, it was almost eight.

"I didn't think you ladies would be coming back in tonight." Fred said as they sat at the counter.

"We did a little shopping before coming in. Can you play my mix tonight?" Hailey asked.

"That depends on what's on it." Fred leaned against the counter.

"It's a mix, Uncle Fred. There are oldies, country, the blues, hip hop, rock, and tons of other types of music on it. But mostly songs we can dance to." Hailey walked behind the counter and threw an arm around her uncle. "Please. I want to spend the night dancing with my friends."

Chapter 13

"Why are we stopping here?" Maverick asked as Dallas pulled into the parking lot in front of Fred's Bar.

"I think that is Hailey's car." Dallas said as he parked. "I am going to see my wife."

Maverick and Jayden followed Dallas inside. Loud music was playing, and the place was packed. He had never seen the place so lively. Maverick moved to the counter while Dallas scanned the room as he slowly followed.

"Busy night." Maverick commented and Fred nodded his head in agreement.

"Word got out that the three karaoke girls were back. Now everyone is here for the show." Fred shook his head. "Not that the ladies know it. They are in their own little world, having the time of their lives."

Maverick looked at the dance floor and saw three women in cowgirl boots, short jean shorts, matching plaid shirts in different colors, and cowgirl hats. The smaller one sat on a bar stool that had been moved to the far side of the dance floor where a standing table sat.

The other two were of similar height. One had brown hair that reached halfway down her back, the other had golden blonde hair that barely reached her shoulders. Their hats shielded their faces, making it impossible to see who they were. They were currently dancing to 'Havanna' by Camila Cabello.

Maverick fully turned to see them better. They were singing and dancing to the music with their backs toward him. He turned his attention to the other occupants at the bar. Most of them were men who were watching the three women with smiles. Maverick's hackles rose. These guys had no business ogling the women.

"How much have they had to drink?" Jayden laughed as he watched them.

"They are on their seventh round of Dr. Pepper and Pepsi." Fred laughed. "Not a drop of alcohol in them."

"I don't see her, but her scent is everywhere." Dallas whispered. Maverick knew he was referring to Hailey.

"Why don't we find a seat and wait a bit? Maybe she is in the bathroom." Jayden suggested.

The three brothers found a small table in a far corner after getting some sodas. Maverick found that his attention kept returning to the women across the room. The smaller one remained sitting while the other two would periodically move a little away from their table before dancing. They would always hug each other after as they laughed.

"I thought you were interested in Morgan?" Dallas snapped his fingers in front of Maverick's face to get his attention.

"I am." Maverick scowled at his brother.

"I noticed you staring at them, and you are married." Jayden laughed as he shoved Dallas's shoulder.

"I am looking for Hails." Dallas defended himself.

"I haven't heard this song in ages." Jayden laughed when 'Over You' by Daughtry started blaring through the speakers.

Maverick watched as all three women sang at the top of their lungs. The blonde's hat fell off as one of her friends hugged her and Maverick froze. He couldn't seem to breathe as he watched Morgan pour her heart into the song as she sang with her eyes closed.

"That's Morgan!" Jayden nearly yelled. "Do you think she is singing this song about you, Mav? She looks like she means every word."

Maverick couldn't pull his eyes away from her. "I sure hope not."

"Who is she with?"

"Let's watch for a while to see what kind of reception Maverick is going to have and keep an eye out for Hailey." Dallas chuckled.

The song ended and another familiar song came on and Maverick swallowed hard. This song would forever remind him of Morgan. She wasn't the only one singing it this time. The other two were equally enthusiastic about it.

'Halo' by Beyonce was the next song and the other two girls with Morgan shoved her away from the table as they laughed. Morgan shook her head as she settled her hat back in place. She slipped her boots off. She began dancing and Maverick was speechless. The song was half over when her friend joined her, and Morgan flicked the other woman's hat off. Hailey. Dallas and Maverick both stood and started making their way slowly through the crowded bar.

*   *   *

'Over You' started to play and Sally did a fist pump. "Okay, so I know I changed your theme song away from this one now that you are getting over Luke, but for old time's sake you should sing it."

"Don't tell me you two are still doing the theme song game." Hailey laughed as Sally cheered. Morgan groaned.

"More like a curse." Morgan whined.

"Please." Sally begged. "I'll sing it with you."

Morgan relented and put her whole heart into it. Hailey hugged her while they sang, causing Morgan's hat to fall off. This song had helped her process Luke's cheating. 'Meant to Be' by Bebe Rexha came on next and all three of them sang it as loud as they could; Morgan taking the female part while Sally and Hailey sang the male part.

"Oh my gosh! I changed my mind. This is your theme song!" Sally bounced in her chair when 'Halo' by Beyonce started to play.

"No, Sal. Please don't do this to me." Morgan begged.

Sally started shoving her. "You have to sing it." She laughed manically. "It's the rules."

"I want to see you own it." Hailey joined in and Morgan shook her head. "You have to, it's the rules."

Morgan glared at them as she took two steps back. She took her boots off and tossed them under their table. "Fine, but I am singing it to you two, not the whole bar."

"You still dance?" Hailey asked excitedly.

"It's how I coped with everything over the years. Morgan shrugged.

Sally and Hailey clapped as they turned to watch her. Morgan kept her back facing the bar as she closed her eyes and took a deep breath. An image of Maverick popped up in her mind and she opened her eyes as she began to sing, putting in as much feeling as she could. She pretended she was alone in a ballet studio and danced.

Halfway through the song, Hailey joined her on the dance floor and Morgan flipped Hailey's hat off, causing her to stick her tongue out at Morgan before she retrieved her hat from the ground. Hailey had taken lessons with Morgan for years. The two of them finished the song dancing an old routine they had done for a recital.

They returned to their table and Sally clapped with a huge smile on her face. "Okay, that is definitely your theme song."

"Ha ha, just wait until I find your new song, little sister." Morgan warned with a smile as she pulled on her boots.

They were all laughing when a man came up behind Hailey, spinning her around. She gasped in surprise, but as soon as she looked up at the man, she squealed and threw her arms around his neck.

"Dallas! I didn't expect you to be back so soon." Hailey said before kissing him.

"We didn't either. I saw your car in the parking lot and decided to stop." Dallas placed another kiss on Hailey's lips. 'I Cross My Heart' by George Strait began to play. "Dance with me, Sweetheart." Dallas pulled Hailey onto the dance floor.

Morgan turned to watch her friend and her heart nearly stopped. Maverick stood in front of her. "May I have this dance?" he asked, holding out his hand.

Morgan swallowed hard as her gaze locked with his. He gently grabbed her hand as Sally pulled Morgan's hat off her head. Maverick slowly walked backwards a few steps while keeping eye contact with her.

Maverick kept her right hand in his left as he wrapped his other arm around Morgan's waist, drawing her closer. She placed her free hand on his shoulder and closed her eyes as he began swaying. She followed his lead. Halfway through the song, Maverick pulled her closer to him as he brought their joined hands to his chest.

Morgan found herself relaxing against him. She slid her hand down his arm as she rested her head on his shoulder. The song was coming to an end, and Morgan dreaded it. She wanted to stay where she was.

'Kick The Dust Up' by Luke Bryan began to play, and Morgan was pulled from Maverick's arms. She was spun around to face Hailey. "You promised, Morgan. This is a must."

"Hails, Morgan and I need to talk." Maverick said from behind them.

"But she promised me this dance." Hailey put her hands on her hips. "You can talk after. This is not up for debate."

Hailey pulled Morgan to the bar and leaned over the counter. She grabbed her phone and restarted the song before pulling Morgan back to the dance floor, away from everyone. They started the line dance and Morgan found herself smiling again.

As soon as the song ended, Hailey pulled Morgan into a tight hug. "Sally can ride home with me and Dallas." Hailey slipped Morgan's car keys into her hand.

"Thanks." Morgan gave Hailey a half smile.

"Give him hell, girl." Hailey winked before going back to where Sally sat.

Morgan felt Maverick move up behind her. He grabbed her hand and she turned to him. "Can we please talk?"

"Sure." Morgan gave a small nod.

He tightened his hand on hers as he pulled her down the hall where the bathrooms were. A metal door was at the end of the hall and Maverick pushed through it. He released her and took a deep breath. He started to talk, but Morgan held up her hand, cutting him off.

Morgan turned and walked towards the parking lot. She heard Maverick following after her. She reached her truck and pulled open the door and climbed in.

"We need to talk, Morgan." Maverick said again.

"I am not having this conversation here. So, you can either get in or stay here. Either way, I'm leaving." Morgan said as she closed the door and started the engine.

Maverick jogged to the other side of the car and jumped in. Morgan didn't even look in his direction. When Maverick started to speak again, Morgan turned on the radio. Maverick sat back and glared out the window as she drove to the field. It only took ten minutes, but she could tell that Maverick was frustrated. Good, so was she.

She parked out of sight of the road and climbed out. The wind blew and she shivered. Short sleeves and short shorts weren't exactly ideal for the chilly nights.

Maverick walked around the hood of the truck and began pacing in front of her. Morgan leaned against the side of the truck and watched him. She waited for several minutes for him to say something, but he remained quiet. All he did was run his hand through his hair a few times as he paced.

"Why, Maverick? Why didn't you just ask me about Taz?" Morgan asked angrily, breaking the silence.

Maverick whirled around to face her. "I know I messed up, Morgan."

"I didn't ask you if you knew you messed up, I asked you why." Morgan folded her arms as another breeze blew through the clearing.

"My little brother went missing, and we were sent to find him. I noticed Jayden's scent on your sock. Then it was strongest wherever you were or had recently been." Maverick raked his hand through his hair. "We knew that he had to be with you."

"You could have just asked about him, Maverick." Morgan felt the sting of tears. It was what she feared, he was just using her.

"It's not that simple." Maverick growled.

"Oh really? Because from where I am standing, it is." Morgan fumed. "I had information you wanted. You decided the best way to get said info, was to get close to me. Well, it worked, Maverick. I led you straight to him."

Maverick's eyes widened in surprise before he took a step towards her. "It wasn't like that."

"Then explain it to me, Maverick." Morgan threw her arms out to the side as her frustration built.

"From the moment you told me I was going to have to work for it, I knew you were going to be worth every second. Morgan, please believe me." Maverick took another small step towards her. "I knew Jayden was safe with you. And knowing that, my focus quickly changed from finding him to getting to know you. I knew that eventually I would need to tell my brother to go home, but I wasn't in a rush to leave."

Morgan studied Maverick for any signs of deceit but didn't see any. "Are these feelings coming from the mate bond, or did you actually care about me?"

Maverick became very still. She watched him closely. He swallowed hard. "You know we are mates?" His voice became less earnest and more guarded.

"I wasn't completely sure until now. Were you even going to tell me?" Morgan wrapped her arms around herself to try to get warm.

"I wasn't sure how." Maverick admitted, rubbing the back of his neck.

"If it wasn't for the mate bond, would you be standing here trying to set things right." Morgan asked.

Maverick met her eyes. "If I were human and the mate bond wasn't a factor, I would still be here, standing in front of you, begging you to forgive me."

Morgan shivered as the wind blew again. She couldn't stand it anymore. She was freezing. She turned around and opened the door to her truck to look for a jacket. An arm snaked around her waist and pulled her from the truck before the door was slammed shut.

Maverick spun her around as he put his hand on the back of her head and pushed her up against the truck. If his hand hadn't been there, her head would have smacked the window. He looked down at her with a pained expression.

"Please don't leave." Maverick whispered.

Morgan blinked in surprise before biting her lip to keep from smiling. "I wasn't leaving, Maverick. I'm cold and was hoping to find a jacket." Maverick let out a tense breath as he rested his forehead against hers. They stood there for several minutes. Morgan shivered again. "I'm still freezing, Maverick." She whispered.

Maverick kissed her forehead before stepping back and opening the cab door. "You said it was in here?" he asked, leaning in.

"I sure hope it is." Morgan rubbed her arms, trying to warm up.

Maverick closed the door before turning to her. He unfolded a blanket and wrapped it around her. "Sorry, no jacket. All I found was a blanket." He wrapped his arms around her as well and she pressed closer to him. He rubbed her arms when she shivered again.

"So, you were saying something about begging?" Morgan said, pulling the blanket tighter around her.

She felt Maverick chuckle. "Whatever I need to do, Baby. Just say the word and I'll do it. Whatever you want, I'll get it."

Morgan remained silent as she thought. She could hear his heart beating wildly where she rested her head on his chest. They stood in silence, and she knew he was waiting for her to say something.

Morgan leaned back so she could see his face. He looked down at her with pleading blue eyes. His hair was disheveled from the multiple times he had run his hands through it.

"I can't do this." Morgan whispered in frustration.

She couldn't keep her distance anymore. She wanted to kiss him. She wanted a future with him. Pain and disappointment filled Maverick's eyes before he closed them. He took a deep breath and slowly let it out.

Morgan raised up on her toes and pressed her lips to his. He tensed for a second before returning the kiss. He tangled his fingers in her hair as he deepened the kiss. Morgan lowered back on her feet after several minutes. She took a step back. Maverick watched her with a confused expression.

"That better not have been a good-bye kiss." Maverick said and his jaw clenched.

"Not really my style." Morgan shrugged as she took another step back. Maverick tracked her movement closely.

"So, where do we stand?" Maverick asked.

"Under the stars." Morgan said with a smirk.

Maverick narrowed his eyes at her. "I'm aware we are under the stars."

Morgan took another step back. She was almost to the back of the truck. She was hoping to get around it before Maverick reached her. She wanted to tease him a little and then do a little stargazing. Maverick matched her step and her heart accelerated. His head cocked to the side.

"Has anyone ever told you not to run from a predator?" Maverick asked as he smiled, taking a step forward and she took one back.

"I think I have heard that somewhere." She said slowly. "But that advice only works if you don't want to get caught." Morgan turned and sprinted for the agility course. She could hear Maverick right behind her.

She jumped over a low jump. Morgan heard Maverick trip and fall over it as she vaulted over a small wall before diving behind the tunnel. Morgan laid down and looked up at the stars breathing hard.

It wasn't long before Maverick was lying next to her with a smile on his face. He rolled to his side so he could look at her. He cupped her face and stroked her cheek with his thumb. He leaned down and pressed his lips lightly to hers.

"I love you." He whispered against her lips.

Morgan put her arms around Maverick's neck as she kissed him. Maverick's hand traveled down her body, resting on her hip. He pulled back and rested his forehead against hers.

"Baby, you dropped your blanket." He whispered. "We should get you back before you get too cold."

"I could always just use the blanket again." Morgan smiled.

Maverick pressed a quick kiss to her lips. "I want you in something with longer sleeves and longer pants."

Morgan scrunched her nose. "You don't like my outfit?" she asked in surprise.

"The opposite actually. You look amazing. I just don't like all the other guys looking at you." Maverick rubbed the tip of his nose against hers causing Morgan to laugh. "Do you realize how many men were drooling over you? That outfit and dancing like you were...Baby, the only time you get to do that, is when you are with me."

Morgan laughed harder. "Is that so?" Morgan asked. "Last I checked, I didn't belong to you."

Maverick growled. "That is something I am hoping to rectify really soon."

"What are you saying?" Morgan ran her fingers through his hair.

"I want to make you mine, Morgan." Maverick said seriously as he smoothed her hair back from her face. "My best friend. My wife. My everything."

Morgan's breath caught in her lungs. She looked into his eyes as she swallowed. "Your wife?" her breath came out airy.

"If you need more time, I understand. I just want to lay all my cards on the table." Maverick pressed a kiss to her cheek. "I love you and want to marry you."

Morgan shivered and Maverick jumped to his feet, pulling her with him. He kissed her one more time before heading for the truck. He opened the passenger door for her, and she wordlessly climbed in. Maverick started the truck and turned the heater up all the way.

"Where to, Baby?" Maverick asked as Morgan slid across the bench and cuddled up to his side.

Chapter 14

Morgan still hadn't said anything except for their destination by the time they walked into Fred's Bar. Maverick kept her hand firmly in his as they made their way to the back where his brothers and her sister were sitting. They had pulled another table over so that there was room for everyone.

Hailey was the first to see that they had returned and smiled at them. "I see you are still in one piece, Mav. I have to say I am a little disappointed you didn't give him a black eye, Morgan."

"Hey, that's your brother-in-law you are wishing harm to." Dallas pulled her back to him with a growl.

"And I would have deserved it." Maverick said with a smile.

"You sure did. Especially after everything Morgan has been through before. I mean Luke getting mad because she refused to sl..." Hailey's voice started to rise.

"Hailey Marie Knight!" Morgan slapped her hand over her friend's mouth. "I will rip your tongue out." Morgan warned.

"It's Hailey Marie Storm." Hailey pulled Morgan's hands off her face before sticking her tongue out at her.

Maverick pulled Morgan away from Hailey. "You two seem familiar with one another."

"Morgan here is my bestie. From the time we could walk, until we turned sixteen, and her parents took her away from me."

"Wait, this is your friend that taught you about...?" Maverick said as he laughed.

"That is correct. I even helped raise Sally until they left." Hailey shrugged. "Small world."

"Excuse me. May I have this dance?" Maverick turned to see a man with brown eyes and light brown hair. He was smiling at Morgan as he waited for her answer.

"Miles?" Morgan laughed before hugging the man. Maverick clenched his jaw. "Yeah sure. I can do a dance."

Maverick watched Morgan as she danced with Miles. He crossed his arms over his chest as he fought the urge to cut in. Hailey and Dallas gave him a sympathetic look while Jayden and Sally were laughing. Morgan was practically glowing as she smiled at Miles. Maverick was not happy.

*   *   *

"How did you end up in Maple Grove?" Morgan asked.

"We were traveling to Jeffersonville for a...conference, but our car blew a tire. It can't get repaired until tomorrow. The guy at the desk of the hotel mentioned Fred's was a good place to spend an evening. We walked in and I saw you. Figured I would say hi." Miles smiled at her.

"Sorry about your car."

"I'm not." Miles shrugged. "I've been curious to know how everything panned out with you. Is that the guy? The one glaring at us?"

Morgan glanced over Miles's shoulder and saw that Maverick was indeed glaring at them. "Yeah, that's him." Morgan's smile grew. "We are working things out." Morgan said.

"I'm glad to hear it." Miles laughed. "But I will beg a favor from you." There was a mischievous glint in his eye.

"And what's that?" Morgan asked suspiciously.

"Make sure he knows I'm not a threat."

Morgan laughed so hard they stopped dancing. Miles led her back over to Maverick. She was still smiling when she made the introductions.

"Maverick, this is Miles. Miles this is Maverick." Morgan glanced at Maverick. His arms were folded over his chest, and he was scowling.

"Nice to finally meet you." Miles said as he extended his hand for a handshake.

Maverick grudgingly shook Miles's hand after several awkward seconds. "How do you know Morgan?"

"I had the pleasure of meeting Morgan a few weeks ago at the beach. Though she didn't look this cute then. I love what you did with your hair, by the way." Miles draped his arm over her shoulders. That mischievous glint sparked in his eyes again as he looked down at Morgan and winked before looking back at Maverick. "I saw her swimming with her dog in that cute little pink bikini and asked her out for ice cream."

Morgan saw Maverick tense. "For a guy who doesn't want to be seen as a threat, you are digging your own grave, and I am not helping you out of it." Morgan hissed close to his ear before stepping back. She turned to face everyone as they watched her. "Sally made me promise to go out with the first guy that asked, and ice cream seemed painless enough." Morgan narrowed her eyes at Miles, who was grinning ear to ear.

"Oh, come on, that wasn't a date. You were so mentally checked out. I think you only said one word the whole time and that was vanilla." Miles laughed.

Maverick remained tense and Morgan moved a little closer to him. His arm went around her waist and he pulled her close to his side. Miles's eyes dropped to Maverick's hand.

Miles winked at Morgan again. "I hope to see you again before I leave tomorrow. Wanna meet up for breakfast?"

Maverick's hand tightened on her hip. "Sure, we will meet you at Maive's Diner at nine?"

"Sounds great." Miles answered before walking away.

Maverick pulled Morgan into his arms. "You are going on a date with him?" he whispered close to her ear. He sounded ticked.

"No, *we* are going to meet up with a friend for breakfast." Morgan wrapped her arms around his neck. "He was messing with you, Maverick. Now are you just going to stand here and glare at him or are you going to ask me to dance?"

Maverick finally looked at her. He kissed her forehead before pulling her onto the dance floor. They danced to several more songs before she saw Sally and Jayden dancing. As the night wore on, Maverick kept Morgan close.

Morgan noticed Sally sitting at the table. She was rubbing her leg with a grimace on her face.

"Maverick, I need to get my sister home." Morgan turned her worried eyes to him. "She doesn't look like she is doing very well."

Maverick's head snapped in Sally's direction. Mid-song, he grabbed her hand and led her to Sally. They let Hailey know they were leaving, and Morgan helped Sally get her crutches. Maverick walked them out to Morgan's truck. Sally winced when she climbed into the back seat.

"Is flyboy coming too?" Sally yawned.

Morgan turned back to Maverick. She did not want him to go but knew he couldn't stay the whole night. Morgan bit her lip in indecision.

"Baby, I will do whatever you want me to do." Maverick said softly.

"Will you drive?" Morgan asked. Maverick smiled as he opened the door for her.

*   *   *

Morgan settled on the couch next to Maverick. She had changed into her pajamas and a sweatshirt as soon as she made sure Sally got in bed. Maverick wrapped his arms around her, and she snuggled up against him.

"Let me know when you want to go to bed, and I will head home." Maverick said as he kissed her head. Morgan snuggled closer and took a deep breath. She wished he didn't need to leave. "Morgan?"

Morgan sighed and sat up. "You should probably leave now then."

"You don't sound too sure about that." Maverick watched her closely.

Morgan shook her head and looked at the blank TV. Maverick gently took her face in his hands and forced her to look at him. "Baby, talk to me."

Morgan closed her eyes. Maverick brushed his thumb across her cheek before brushing a light kiss to her lips. "The past several weeks have been so hard." Morgan whispered.

"I'm sorry." Maverick rubbed the tip of his nose against hers. "What made it so hard?"

Morgan sat back and glared at him. "You did."

"Me?"

"Yes, you." Morgan laid her head on his shoulder and pulled her legs up under her. "I was so mad at you. And I missed you."

"I missed you too, Baby." Maverick kissed her brow. "Why didn't you answer my calls?" he asked.

"What calls?" Morgan asked confused.

"I called at least twice a day the whole time you were gone."

"Sally wanted to go off grid for the first two weeks while we were at the beach, so we turned off the phone. But I haven't received any calls or texts since we turned it back on, other than from Missy." Morgan pulled her phone from her hoodie pocket. "See." She showed Maverick the call history.

Maverick took the phone from her and scrolled through it. Sure enough, there was no record of him calling her. He checked to see if his number was blocked. It was. He unblocked his number, saved it to her contacts, and handed Morgan back her phone.

"Sally said an unknown number kept calling and must have blocked it." Morgan shook her head. "I am so sorry. If I had known you were calling, I would have answered."

"Would you have?" Maverick asked. "I wouldn't blame you if you didn't. I was an idiot for how I handled everything."

"You will get no argument from me there." Morgan laughed.

Maverick chuckled before kissing her. When he tried to break the kiss off, Morgan pulled him back to her. He smiled against her lips and Morgan deepened the kiss.

"Morgan, can I get some more pain med...Oh!" Sally's voice called before cutting off.

Morgan gasped, pulling away from Maverick as she felt her cheeks heat. "Umm...yes, they are in the kitchen. Did you want me to get them for you?" Morgan asked trying to slow down her rapidly beating heart.

"I can get them. You seem busy." Sally smiled before slowly making her way to the kitchen. Maverick chuckled when Morgan buried her face in his chest. "You know, I don't think I have ever seen you kiss anyone before. Well except once, but it was a small peck." Sally said loudly from the kitchen.

Morgan groaned softly before sitting up. "I thought you were asleep." Morgan started to say.

"That's obvious." Sally came back in the room. "I'm not a little kid anymore, Morgan. I know that when two people are in love they kiss and stuff, you know the whole birds and the bees thing."

"Sally." Morgan said. "You know this family's rule."

"No shenanigans until after marriage, I know. So, when are you getting married? I think I should be the first to know since I will be living with you two." Sally stopped at the doorway of her room and looked at them. Morgan bit her lip. "He has asked you, hasn't he?"

"Kind of." Morgan said slowly as Maverick's arms tightened around her.

Maverick's phone started to ring. He fished it out of his pocket. "Hello." Morgan heard a male voice from the other end of the call but couldn't make out what was said. "Can't Dallas do it?" Maverick's body tensed as he listened. "If you know she just got back, why are you calling me in?" Maverick's fingers started to rub Morgan's arm slowly. "Fine. I'll be there in an hour." Maverick hung up the phone and ran his hand down his face.

"What's wrong?" Morgan asked.

"Someone breeched our pack border. Two of our men were injured in a scuffle. My dad is calling us all in to up security and figure out how to keep our pack safe from future attacks." Maverick looked down at her.

"It's the middle of the night, do you have to go now?" Morgan asked, surprised at how needy she sounded.

"If I could stay, I would, but the attack came from the Maple Grove border. Dad believes it was some of the locals here. Things have been escalating quickly over the last few months and something has to be done before someone gets killed." Maverick stood and stretched his shoulders.

Morgan got to her feet and followed him to the door. "You will be careful?" Morgan asked.

Maverick turned back to her and smiled. "Always." He pulled her to him before kissing her. "Take Sally with you when you meet up with that Miles guy. I don't want him getting any ideas."

Morgan laughed. "Give me my ring and I won't need a chaperone." She raised her brow in challenge.

"A ring would mean you are agreeing to be my wife." Maverick became serious as he looked down at her.

"I am aware of what accepting a ring from a man means, Maverick." Morgan smiled at Maverick's surprised expression. He slowly reached into his pocket and pulled out a small box, and Morgan gasped. She hadn't expected him to actually have a ring yet. "Maverick." Her voice was barely louder than a whisper.

"I got it about a month ago." Maverick smiled at her look of surprise. "You sure about this, Baby? Once my ring is on your finger, I fully intend to have a short engagement." Maverick watched her closely.

Morgan lifted her eyes from the box in Maverick's hand until their gazes met. She narrowed her eyes. "How short?"

Maverick took a small step forward so that they were only inches apart. "A week or two."

"So long?" Morgan breathed out, causing Maverick to laugh.

Maverick pulled the ring from the box and slipped it on her finger. She stared down at it as her stomach did a somersault. It was stunning. The diamond was set in a white gold band. It was simple but she loved it. Having the diamond in the band would reduce the risk of it catching on things while she worked with the dogs.

Morgan returned her gaze to Maverick's face. She wrapped her arms around his neck and pressed her lips to his. "I love you." She whispered against his lips. The moment the words came from her mouth, Maverick kissed her more fervently as he pressed her against the wall.

"Ok, you love each other. We get it." Sally said while making gagging noises behind them.

Morgan laughed and Maverick smiled. "I will be back as soon as I can." He kissed her one more time before he took a step back. "This time, Baby, answer my calls." He winked at her before shifting into a large grey wolf, his blue eyes standing out against the white fur on his face.

He took off running into the trees and Morgan sagged against the door jam. She missed him already. Sighing, Morgan went back inside and closed the door slowly. When she turned around, Sally was grinning ear to ear.

"He is cute," Sally moved to sit by Morgan. "And he adores you."

"So, you like him?" Morgan asked her sister. "And you are okay with this?" Morgan lifted her left-hand, showing it to Sally.

Sally grabbed her hand and studied the ring. "He adores you, glares at any man that looks at you, protects you, and he respects you." Sally tapped the ring. "He knows you well enough to get you a ring that you can wear while working. He even puts your needs above his own. And most importantly, he makes you happy, Morgan." Sally cuddled up to Morgan's side. "I am happy for you."

Morgan wrapped her arms around her sister and held her close. She was happy. Happy that she had found Hailey. Happy that her sister was there with her. Happy that she had Maverick in her life.

Chapter 15

Banging at the front door startled Morgan and Sally awake. Morgan jumped up off the couch where they had fallen asleep and ran to the door. She pulled the door open and froze. She had expected to see Maverick, but instead, Devon and Jake stood on her front porch.

"Are you okay?" Jake asked.

Morgan furrowed her brow in confusion. "Yes. Why wouldn't I be?" Morgan asked, crossing her arms over her chest.

"Over the last couple weeks, we have noticed an increase of wolf activity around here and you haven't been to work in a while." Devon said as he tried to see around her. "And Eli told us you were staying here."

Morgan stepped outside and pulled the door closed. "Why would wolves in the forest affect me? And why are you watching me?"

"These aren't normal wolves." Jake insisted. "That dog you insisted on keeping hidden was not even a dog, but a werewolf. They are dangerous."

"We have game cameras set up near the borders of the Winter's property and they are picking up more and more wolves coming here." Devon added.

"When did you put cameras up on my land?" Morgan stiffened.

"Your land? No, this property belongs to the Winters. We set them up a few months ago, after that werewolf came to town." Jake put his hands on his hips.

"I bought this cabin and the surrounding four hundred acres months ago. I will give you two hours to remove the cameras, or I will." Morgan threatened.

"What part of werewolves do you not understand?" Devon grabbed her arm and yanked her to him. "They are vermin and need to be taken care of."

He tightened his grip on her, and she winced. "Werewolves are not dangerous. They are just people like you and me." Morgan said through clenched teeth. Devon's hold was becoming painful, and she tried to step away, but he wouldn't release her. "Let go of me, Devon." Morgan snapped. She cried out as his hand tightened again. It felt like a tourniquet.

"You obviously can't be left here alone since you aren't taking this threat seriously." Devon took a few steps toward the stairs with Morgan trying to break his painful grip.

"Let go of my sister." Sally's voice came from behind Morgan.

Morgan turned to see Sally aiming their handgun at Devon. Devon slowly released Morgan's arm and raised his hands in a show of surrender. Morgan moved to Sally's side and took the gun from her before turning her attention back to their unwanted visitors.

"Get off my property. You come back and I will not hesitate to defend myself, my home, and my family." Morgan glared at the men. "Consider your cameras lost."

They slowly backed off the porch and climbed into their car. Morgan stayed on the porch, watching them until they drove out of sight. She locked the door as soon as she was back inside.

"Maverick is going to be pissed." Sally warned.

"He isn't Devon and Jake's biggest fan, but them showing up here isn't going to make him that mad." Morgan walked towards her room.

"I was referring to your arm." Sally called after her. Morgan looked down to where Devon had grabbed her. It was red and tender. She hoped it wouldn't bruise.

*   *   *

Morgan pulled into the parking lot of the diner a little after nine. She parked her motorcycle near the door and headed inside. She looked around the room until she saw Miles sitting at a booth near the back. She walked quickly as she unzipped her bike jacket. Morgan dropped her helmet and jacket on the bench before plopping down.

"Good morning." Miles greeted her with a smile.

"Good morning." Morgan forced a smile. This morning wouldn't be one of her better mornings.

"Where is Maverick? I thought for sure he wouldn't let you anywhere near me without him at your side." Miles sat back and glanced at the door.

"He got called away on business and my little sister's leg is hurting her, so she stayed at home." Morgan shrugged. She wished she could have talked with Maverick about what happened this morning before coming, but after Devon and Jake left, Morgan had barely enough time to get dressed before she needed to leave.

Maive brought over glasses of water and took their order. "It looks like congratulations are in order." Miles nodded to Morgan's hand and the ring.

"Thank you." Morgan smiled as she ran her finger along the ring.

"Did he give you that too?" Morgan glanced up at Miles to see him gesture to her arm. Morgan looked down and could see that bruises were starting to appear where Devon had grabbed her.

"Of course not. This was from..." Morgan started to explain when her phone rang. She glanced at the screen and saw Maverick's name. "Sorry, I need to get this." She said quickly as she answered the call. "Hello."

"Good morning, Baby." Maverick's voice brought a smile to her face.

"Good morning. How are things going?"

Maverick sighed. "I am just about to head into a meeting. Actually, I am already late, but I wanted to talk with you first. Once the meeting starts, I will be unreachable for a few hours."

"I'm glad you called." Morgan turned a little away from the table. "Something happened this morning."

"I will be right there, Dallas. Just give me a few minutes." Maverick said. "Go on, Baby."

Morgan took a deep breath before continuing. "I love you Maverick, but I need your full attention for like two minutes."

"I love you too." She could hear the smile in Maverick's voice. "Dallas give me back my phone."

"Sorry to have to do this to you, Morgan, but we really do need to go." Dallas came on the line.

"Dallas, this is important. Give Maverick back the phone." Morgan snapped, but she could tell Dallas wasn't listening. He and Maverick were yelling at each other before the line went dead.

Morgan growled and tried to call Maverick back, but it went straight to voice mail. She dropped her phone on the table in frustration. On the drive over, Morgan had a thought. If Devon and Jake had placed several game cameras along the border of her property to keep tabs on wolf activity, were they the ones attacking Maverick's pack? Were they using the cameras to know where and when to strike? Maverick had mentioned that attacks were coming more frequently over the last several months and the cameras were set up a few months ago. It couldn't be a coincidence.

"Do I want to know what that is about?" Miles asked.

Morgan looked up and sighed. "I think I might have a lead on who is attacking a friend of mine's community." Morgan rubbed her temples. She could feel the start of a headache coming on.

"Want to talk about it?" Miles offered in a softer voice.

"This really isn't the place to talk about this." Morgan sat back and studied Miles. He was a really nice guy and proving to be a good friend and listening ear but she wasn't sure if she fully trusted him.

Morgan's phone started to ring again. Maverick's name flashed on the screen. She picked it up. "You have a lot of nerve, Dallas. You can't just take someone's phone from them and hang up. That kind of behavior is not okay." Morgan fumed.

There was a brief pause before a deep voice spoke. "My name is Connor Storm. I am the Alpha of the Maple Grove Pack." Morgan blinked in surprise, not the person she had thought would be calling her. "Are you the human, Morgan Elliot?"

Morgan bristled. "I am a person just like you are." Morgan said icily. "Now, I would like to talk with Maverick."

"We are currently in a meeting, Ms. Elliot. I just wanted you to know that this meeting is important, and that Maverick is required to be here." Connor responded.

"I understand the importance of this meeting." Morgan said as calmly as she could. She wasn't an idiot who needed things spelled out for her. "You and all the other prominent members of your communities could learn to exercise a little patience. I have something important to say to Maverick and it cannot wait."

"This meeting can't wait." Connor stated firmly.

"Is someone currently dying?"

"No."

"Is there an immediate threat knocking at your door?"

"No, but..."

"Is someone there that means you harm?

"No."

"Ms. Elliot!" The Sheriff yelled as he stomped in her direction.

"What now?" Morgan snapped.

"Ms. Elliot, I need you to under..." Connor started to say, but the Sheriff reached her side.

"Ms. Elliot, we need to talk." The Sheriff demanded.

"I am on an important phone call, Sheriff Brown, you are just going to have to wait." Morgan glanced up at him and then over at Miles. The sheriff's posture was stiff, and his face was red with anger. Miles looked entertained by everything going on.

"My son said you pulled a gun on him, and he was scared for his life." Sheriff Brown lowered his voice in an effort to keep their conversation private.

"I'm glad. If he was staring down the barrel of a gun and not scared, I would be worried something was even more wrong with him." Morgan commented as she glared up at him.

"Put the phone away and answer my questions or I will be detaining you for questioning. The decision is yours." The Sheriff rested his hand on his firearm.

Morgan watched the movement before looking back at Miles. His look of amusement was gone, and he watched the police officer with a hard expression. He was like a completely different person.

"Look, Mr. Storm, I am going to have to talk with you later. It appears I have to speak with the police about a situation that happened earlier. Tell Dallas to keep his hands off things that don't belong to him and tell Maverick that I really need to speak with him." Morgan ended the call. "What do you want to know?"

"Did you point a gun at Devon and Jake?"

"Yes." Morgan said as she glanced again at Miles. The Sheriff followed her gaze.

"Why don't you come with me outside for a few minutes?" The Sheriff asked, stepping back to give her room to stand.

Morgan grudgingly stood and walked outside. She was sure Maverick wasn't going to be happy about this. Neither would Sally. Anxiety started to fill her veins as worse case scenarios began circling around in her mind. If she was arrested, who would watch out for Sally? Morgan reminded herself that she did nothing wrong, as the door to the diner closed behind her.

*   *   *

Maverick watched as his dad stared down at the phone in his hand. Morgan seemed ticked as she spoke with him. Maverick swallowed as he waited for his dad to say something.

"What did she say?" Jayden got to his feet.

"She said that she had something important to tell Maverick. Then someone started talking with her. She told me she had to go talk to the police. She reprimanded Dallas and reiterated that she needed to talk with Maverick. Then she hung up." Connor took in the room slowly. His gaze finally settled on Maverick, a thoughtful expression on his face. "Call her back." He said as he tossed Maverick the phone.

Maverick didn't waste any time as he hit Morgan's name on his contact list. It rang twice before a male voice answered. "Hello?"

"Who is this?" Maverick asked.

"Maverick? Morgan said you were busy this morning. Something about a meeting."

"Miles?" Maverick's eyes narrowed. "Where is Morgan?"

"Uh. She is currently standing outside the diner talking with a Sheriff Brown. I am watching her from the window." There was a pause. "Not in a creepy or stalker kind of way."

"What is going on?" Maverick asked, getting to his feet and pacing.

"I honestly have no idea. When she got here, she seemed distracted. She said you and her sister couldn't make it for various reasons. I commented on her ring, which made her smile. Congrats, man. I'm happy for the both of you." Miles sounded like he was smiling.

"Thanks, but I want to know more about what is going on with Morgan." Maverick couldn't help the small smile that curved his lips at the mention of his ring on Morgan's finger.

"She got mad when she tried to tell you something, but then someone hung up on her. I think she tried to call you back immediately, but it went straight to voicemail. I asked her if she wanted to talk about what was bothering her, but she got another call. She was not happy with whoever she was talking to. Then the Sheriff showed up. He asked her if she aimed a gun at someone named Devon, and Morgan admitted to it."

Maverick ran a hand down his face. Is that what she had been trying to tell him, that she had to defend herself with a gun? "What is happening now?" He asked Miles. Maverick was frustrated that he wasn't with Morgan at that very moment.

"They are still talking outside. Martinez and I think that the bruising on Morgan's arm came from either Devon or Jake. Both were mentioned in connection to her aiming a gun at them." Miles stated. "I am going to have to let you go, Maverick. Things look to be heating up outside."

"Keep her safe for me." Maverick said as he ran his hands through his hair.

"Will do." Miles said quickly before the call ended.

Maverick continued to pace until Dallas grabbed his arm. "What is going on?"

Maverick pulled free of his brother. "Apparently, Morgan ran into a little trouble this morning." Dallas had a slightly guilty look on his face. "Devon and Jake showed up at the cabin. Miles says the Sheriff asked Morgan about pointing a gun at them and she admitted to it. Miles says he noticed bruising on Morgan's arm. He thinks that either Devon or Jake is responsible for it."

"Maverick, I am so sorry for taking your phone." Dallas said, rubbing the back of his neck.

"Devon is the one that hit Morgan in the face before kicking her in the ribs when she was rescuing me." Jayden got to his feet. "I swear, if they hurt her again..." He growled before storming from the room.

Maverick took a few steps to follow him, but Connor stopped him. "Let Jayden check on her. You can keep your phone on, but we need to get these attacks under control." Connor said firmly.

Dallas gave him a sympathetic look before retaking his seat. Maverick grudgingly followed suit. "If anything happens with Morgan, I am gone." Maverick stated firmly as he clenched his hands into fists under the table. If Morgan was hurt in any way, heads were going to roll.

*   *   *

"I told you, Sheriff, Devon grabbed me and wouldn't let go, even after I asked him to!" Morgan yelled in frustration.

"Someone grabbing you is no reason to pull a gun on them, Ms. Elliot!" Sheriff Brown yelled back.

"I think it is perfectly legal and acceptable for a person to defend themselves with a firearm if their assailant isn't letting them go." Miles said as he and another man walked up to Morgan's side.

"I don't know who you are, but this has nothing to do with you." Sheriff Brown glared at Miles.

"I believe you will find that it does." Miles's friend said as he pulled a leather wallet from his coat pocket. "Agent Garret Martinez from the Federal Bureau of Werewolf and Human Affairs."

Morgan's eyes widened in surprise as Miles pulled out a similar wallet and flashed his own credentials. "I believe you mentioned earlier that Ms. Elliot pulled a gun on your son?" Miles asked.

"She did, on him and his friend." The Sheriff was taken off guard and stared dumbly at the other two men.

"Since the supposed victim is a family member, don't you think that this is a conflict of interest?" Miles asked. "We will be taking over this matter, Sheriff. We will be in touch with your son and his friend following our interview with Ms. Morgan."

The Sheriff opened and closed his mouth several times before turning and storming off towards his patrol car. "Wow. If I had known daring you to ask the cute girl with the scary dog out on a date would lead to this, I would have brought popcorn." Garret said as he smiled at Morgan.

Morgan didn't smile back. She was so angry at the moment. "What is going on, Morgan." Miles asked as he gently touched her arm.

"Not here. Is your car fixed?" Morgan asked.

"I believe the guy said it would be done by ten thirty." Garret said.

Morgan gave them her address and retrieved her jacket and helmet from the diner before heading back to the cabin. She was surprised that Miles worked for the FBWHA. But maybe this was good. Maybe he and Agent Martinez would be able to help her locate the cameras and put an end to the attacks on Maverick's pack.

Chapter 16

Morgan paced her living room while Sally sat on the couch quietly. Morgan had told Sally about what had happened at the diner, and how Miles and Agent Martinez would be stopping by so that she could talk to them about what happened with Devon and Jake.

It was nearly eleven when a knock sounded at the door. Morgan moved to it quickly after grabbing her gun. She wasn't going to let Devon and Jake get the best of her again. Morgan slowly opened the door.

"Taz!" Morgan cried as she put the gun on the side table and yanked open the door. She threw her arms around his neck and gave him a tight hug.

"Maverick was not happy that he couldn't come." Taz hugged her back. "What's been going on here?"

Before Morgan could answer, a car pulled into the clearing. Taz stepped in front of her, shielding her from whoever had just shown up. Morgan heard the sound of car doors closing.

"Can I help you?" Taz called loudly.

"Morgan invited us." Miles called from a good distance away.

Taz was tense. "It's okay, Taz. They are friends." Morgan whispered. She touched Taz's arm softly, as she moved to his side. "Come in gentlemen." Morgan held open the door and the three men walked inside.

"Hey, Taz." Sally greeted him with a smile. "Did Maverick send you?"

"Not exactly, but I was the only person at the meeting that didn't really need to be there. I am sure he would have sent me if I had stayed around long enough for him to issue the order." Taz took his usual chair as he studied the two agents.

"Taz, this is Miles O'Brien and Garret Martinez. Agents, this is Taz." Morgan said as she took a seat.

"Agents?" Taz asked in confusion.

"We work for the FBWHA." Martinez answered. "Ms. Elliot here, seems to be in the thick of something that we have been investigating for years."

"Why don't you start with what happened today." Miles suggested as he moved to an empty chair.

"It actually started a few months ago." Morgan said as she rubbed her temples and squeezed her eyes shut. Her headache was getting worse. She told them about Taz coming to the shelter and the attack. She then recounted this morning's events. "Taz, where exactly are your pack's borders?"

"Most of this side of the pack actually borders your property."

"I think Devon and Jake are using the game cameras they have set up to track the members of the nearby pack." Morgan stated her suspicions.

"So that is where you got the bruises from?" Miles asked, his face as hard as stone. "Devon and Jake confronted you about the werewolf pack and grabbed you."

"Show me." Taz growled.

Morgan rolled her eyes as she lifted her arm and looked at the discoloration. Several flashes of light in her peripheral caused her head to snap up. "Did you just...?"

"Take pictures?" Taz finished her question as he looked at his phone. "Sure did. Maverick is going to be pissed."

"You didn't." Morgan breathed out. A few seconds later her phone began playing 'Highway to the Danger Zone' by Kenny Loggins. "Sally." Morgan glared at her sister, who was grinning ear to ear. She shook her head. "Hey, Maverick." Morgan answered.

"Tell me which one of them touched you!" Maverick roared.

"Calm down." Morgan glared at Taz, who only shrugged.

"Don't tell me to calm down, Babe. I can see his handprint on your arm." Maverick growled.

Maverick was definitely ticked. Morgan took a deep breath. "Everything is under control, Love."

There was a brief pause. "Baby, it's not okay for anyone to hurt you like that." Morgan could tell that Maverick was starting to calm down.

"That's why they found themselves staring down the barrel of my .9mm." Morgan smiled. "I'm not helpless, Maverick."

She heard him take a deep breath and slowly let it out. "I still don't want you alone until those two are no longer a threat to you and Sally."

"We will have someone here with us until you come home." Morgan smiled. It was comforting to know that Maverick was protective of both her and Sally. Morgan's smile dropped from her face. "Maverick, are you still in the meeting?"

"Yeah, after Dad's phone call with you, he said I could keep my phone on me in case something else happened."

"You called, during a meeting with several other packs, just because Taz sent you a picture of my arm?" Morgan covered her mouth.

"Baby, no one here faults me for pausing the meeting because my mate and fiancé was grabbed hard enough to leave bruises." Maverick stated.

"Maverick, listen to me very carefully." Morgan said slowly. "I am fine. Sally is fine. It's not the first time I have been grabbed like that. I have lived through far worse than a little bruise. We have things well under control."

"Morgan..."

"No, Maverick. Apologize for the interruption and get back to the meeting. We will be fine. Call when you are done, okay?" Morgan got to her feet and headed for the kitchen. "One more thing, Maverick."

"What's that, Baby?" Maverick asked.

"I love you." Morgan said with a smile.

Maverick chuckled. "Love you too. Talk to you soon."

*   *   *

Maverick smiled as he returned to his seat. He was still not happy about the bruises on Morgan's arm but talking with her had calmed most of his anger. He glanced around the table and noticed everyone was watching him.

"Well?" Dallas asked.

"Morgan said she was fine and had everything under control." Maverick set his phone down on the table.

"Under control? Someone bruised your girl." Alpha Torrin from the Harvest Moon Pack said angrily.

"Morgan isn't a damsel." Charlie said with a laugh. "She slammed a motorcycle helmet into my face because I didn't do as she asked. She is one tough cookie."

Maverick chuckled as he sat back. "She told me to apologize for interrupting the meeting and for us to continue."

"Are you sure she is okay?" Connor asked.

"No, but she insisted on us continuing and if we don't, I will be in hot water with her, so…let's get this over with." Maverick stated, and several of the men laughed. The sooner this meeting ended, the sooner he could get back to Morgan and know for himself she was okay.

* * *

"I can't believe you sent Maverick a picture of my arm." Morgan came back into the living room and glared at Taz.

"He has the right to know." Taz crossed his arms over his chest.

"I would have told him about it when he called, and he would have seen it when he got back. You caused him to worry over nothing." Morgan shot back at him.

"I wouldn't necessarily call it nothing." Miles spoke up. Morgan turned her glare on him. "Martinez and I have been investigating a group of people who have been actively seeking out and attacking the werewolf population."

"We were on our way to a meeting with a couple other teams to share information when our tire blew. We have been in Oceanview for the last two years looking for leads, but have come up empty, until today." Martinez said with a satisfied smile.

"What is the plan?" Taz asked.

"The first step would be to find and remove the cameras. No cameras mean they cannot see the movement of the pack. The only problem is, I have no idea how many cameras they have out there." Morgan began to pace as she thought out loud. "Miles, you and Martinez head back to town and see if you can find Devon or Jake. Get them to tell you how many cameras we need to find."

"You're taking charge?" Miles laughed.

"She usually gets put in charge." Sally said with a laugh. "Of raising me, captain of her sport teams, asking to take over for the women's self-defense instructor, riding instructor, do I need to go on?"

"I think we get it. Morgan is a natural born leader." Miles chuckled as he got to his feet. "We will go see if we can figure out how many cameras we are looking for. When we return, we can start retrieving them."

Morgan watched as Miles and Martinez climbed into their car and drove away. She was anxious to get the cameras taken down and stop Devon and Jake from hurting anyone else. From what Miles had been saying, Morgan suspected that Devon and Jake were a part of the group the agents were looking for.

Three hours later, Morgan's phone rang. Miles told her they were on their way back. There were twenty cameras on the property, but Devon and Jake refused to tell them where they were located.

"I don't have a map of the land." Morgan paced the kitchen while they waited for Miles and Martinez to arrive.

"I can take them around. If those guys were keeping tabs on the pack, the cameras will be along the boundaries." Taz rubbed the back of his neck. "The only problem is you told Maverick someone would be here with you until Devon and Jake were stopped."

"I'll call Hailey." Morgan grabbed her phone quickly and made the call.

Hailey came immediately. She ran to the cabin in her wolf form in order to cut down travel time, but it still took her an hour. Miles and Martinez decided that Taz would lead them as a wolf, while they followed on Morgan's four-wheelers. They left as soon as Hailey got there.

"So, what is going on exactly? All you said on the phone was that you promised Mav that you wouldn't be alone." Hailey asked when the sound of the four-wheelers faded.

Morgan and Sally filled her in on that morning's events. Hailey stared at them in surprise for several minutes before shaking her head.

"Morgan thinks that Devon and Jake are the ones responsible for the attacks on your pack." Sally concluded.

"What is being done?" Hailey asked.

"Miles and Martinez want to gather all the cameras for evidence. They pulled this morning's surveillance video from my security system of when Devon and Jake showed up. Miles said they are also getting the file from when they attacked me a few months ago. They want as much evidence as they can gather in order to put Devon and Jake behind bars." Morgan kicked her feet up on the coffee table. "I think Miles even mentioned reaching out to your Alpha to get information on the attacks they have been experiencing. He is hoping to connect Devon and Jake to them."

"So, what do we do while the guys are busy?" Hailey asked.

"Pool Party?" Sally suggested with a smile. "Not only would sitting in a pool be refreshing, but I am supposed to spend time in the water for physical therapy. Plus, you should see the pool in the back. It even has a great sound system out there."

* * *

Maverick pulled up in front of the cabin with a sigh. It was getting dark, and he couldn't wait to see Morgan. Dallas had called Maverick when he was halfway to the cabin. He was angry. When he got home, Hailey was gone. He found a note saying she was over at Morgan's house. Since he didn't know where to go, Maverick had to turn around to pick up his brother, which resulted in adding an additional hour to his drive.

When they climbed out of the jeep, loud music could be heard from the back of the house. Dallas looked over at Maverick with a questioning eyebrow raised but Maverick only shrugged. He had no idea what was going on.

The song ended and they heard someone scream. Dallas and Maverick took off running for the back of the house. When they rounded the back corner, they both skidded to a stop.

Sally lay on an inflatable bed in a large pool, laughing. "Hurry up before the next song comes on!" Sally yelled. "Remember no pushing each other off the board this time." Hailey and Morgan were attempting to balance on the diving board. Both were laughing as they got to their feet and another song came on over a stereo system.

Morgan was wearing an aqua blue bikini top with short black board shorts that caused Maverick's mouth to go dry. "Hailey has never worn anything like that. She is usually in a t-shirt and shorts." Dallas whispered. His eyes widened as he watched his wife, who was in a hot pink bikini.

'Every Little Thing' by Russell Dickerson filled the clearing and the girls started to dance as they shared the diving board. Maverick could only watch with his mouth open. Morgan stepped close to the end of the diving board as she danced. After the first verse, she switched spots with Hailey. Neither one stopped swaying their hips. Morgan joined her for the rest of the song. They even did air guitars while leaning back against each other. When the song ended, Sally cheered and cat-called causing Morgan and Hailey to laugh while taking a bow.

"Do you girls ever stop dancing?" Dallas called.

Hailey and Morgan screamed as they whirled around to face Dallas and Maverick. Hailey lost her balance and grabbed onto Morgan to try to prevent herself from falling into the pool. It didn't work, both girls fell into the water with a large splash. Maverick started kicking off his shoes while Dallas laughed and pulled his shirt off.

Morgan coughed and wiped her face when she broke the surface of the water. Sally was laughing so hard she was wheezing. Morgan's eyes landed on Maverick as she looked to where the voice had come from. He had a large grin on his face as he pulled his shirt off. Dallas was already running towards the pool in nothing but his boxers.

Hailey screamed again as Dallas cannonballed right in front of her. Maverick did a front flip and swam under the water until he reached Morgan. Morgan wrapped her arms around his neck as his arms went around her waist.

"I thought I told you; you weren't allowed to dance in something like this without me." Maverick whispered.

"We had been talking about my cowgirl outfit. You said nothing about swimsuits." Morgan smiled before pressing her lips to his in a quick kiss.

"Where is Jayden? He was supposed to be here with you?" Maverick asked looking around.

"We would not have been dancing like that if Jayden was here." Hailey commented as Dallas moved the two of them closer to Morgan and Maverick.

"He is helping Miles and Martinez at the moment." Morgan said as she wrapped her legs around Maverick's waist. His hands moved down her back until they grabbed her thighs.

"Miles is here?" Maverick asked in surprise.

Morgan pressed her lips back to Maverick's. "How did your meeting go?"

"After your phone call with our dad, and then Maverick's call with Miles, all the Alpha's were ready to storm this place to see if you were okay." Dallas said with a smile.

"What? All the Alpha's agreeing on something?" Hailey said in surprise. "I don't think I have ever seen that. Usually there is at least two that don't feel the same as the others."

"Morgan reprimanded an Alpha and then hung up on him." Maverick chuckled. "I think she earned their respect. Then Jayden sent a picture, and everyone was mad." His tone instantly became hard." He gently grabbed Morgan's arm and looked at it. "Babe." Maverick's voice held a warning.

"If you are going to ask her if it was Devon or Jake, it was Devon." Sally entered the conversation. "He was dragging her towards the steps, and I thought they were going to try to shove her in the car."

Maverick turned back to Morgan and cupped her cheek. Morgan brushed his wet hair out of his face and looked into his eyes. Maverick was tense and Morgan could feel his anger building.

"Look at me, Maverick." Morgan whispered as she slowly stroked his cheek. His eyes met hers and she smiled. "I am fine." She kissed him slowly and he began to relax.

"You two do realize that we are still here, right?" Hailey splashed them.

Morgan gasped and pulled back from Maverick, breaking their kiss. Her cheeks heated and she buried her face in Maverick's neck. He chuckled, wrapping his arms back around her before he started walking towards the stairs.

"I think we should take this party inside. We can get you ladies caught up on what happened during the meeting, and you can tell us what has been going on here." Maverick said as he carried Morgan out of the pool.

As soon as they were on dry ground, Morgan tried to put her feet down. Maverick grabbed her thighs, keeping her legs around him. He walked inside and went straight to the master bathroom. He finally set her down.

"I could have walked." Morgan said as she took a step back.

"You aren't walking around outside looking like that." Maverick said as he put his hands on Morgan's hips.

Morgan looked down at herself and then back at Maverick. His well-defined muscles were on full display, causing her to blush. "I am in a swimming suit Maverick, in my own backyard. It's not like I am walking around in my birthday suit in the middle of a mall."

Maverick's eyes darkened as he looked at her. He pulled her against him before kissing her again. He turned and pressed her up against the door. The cold wood caused Morgan to gasp and arch away from it. Maverick pulled her away from the cold surface and put his forehead to hers.

"I am going to go grab my clothes before we…" Maverick swallowed hard. "We really need to set a date, Morgan." he said as he slipped out the door.

Morgan bit her lower lip and smiled. She shook her head and laughed as she got into the shower. Ten minutes later, Morgan stepped from her room dressed in skinny jeans and a tank top. Sally was sitting on the couch with a book while Maverick stood near the window with a beach towel around his waist.

"Shower's free." Morgan said and Maverick turned to look at her. Maverick looked her up and down as he slowly approached. "Don't tell me you disapprove of this outfit too." Morgan smirked.

"I am going to disapprove of every flattering outfit you wear, until you are my wife." Maverick pressed a kiss to her forehead before walking into her room.

Morgan sat on the oversized chair facing the couch and sighed. Sally smiled at her before returning her attention back to her book. "I told you he adores you. Luke never treated you half as good as Maverick does."

Chapter 17

Morgan looked up from her phone when Maverick came into the room. He walked over to her and grabbed her hands. He pulled Morgan to her feet and sat in her chair.

"I was sitting there." Morgan put her hands on her hips and narrowed her eyes.

"Morgan!" Taz yelled as the front door banged open and he came storming into the cabin followed by Miles and Martinez. All three of them looked angry.

"Is something wrong?" Maverick was instantly on his feet, standing between Morgan and the three angry men.

"You can say that." Miles said flatly. "But let's all sit down and then we can talk."

Maverick retook his seat and pulled Morgan down onto his lap. He wrapped his arms around her, pressing a kiss to her shoulder. Taz sat on the couch next to Sally while Miles and Martinez sat on other chairs.

"What is going on?" Morgan asked, completely confused as to why everyone was angry.

"When were you planning on telling us who your parents were?" Martinez asked.

Morgan's brows furrowed in confusion. Sally looked at Morgan, equally confused. "What do our parents have to do with anything?" Sally asked.

"Our parents died four years ago in a boating accident." Morgan said.

"Your mother and stepfather died in a boating accident." Miles corrected. "We want to know about your birth father."

"What are you talking about?" Morgan asked. "Our parents were Joseph and Charolette Elliot. Joseph was a drunk who took to physical violence when he mixed his drinks with pills. When Sally came along, he flat out ignored us, leaving me to raise Sally from the time I was nine." She began to grow irritated.

Thoughts of her father always caused Morgan to get angry. He hadn't been a good man. She had found herself his target most of the time when he got in one of his moods. Mom would sit on the couch and watch, too high or drunk to care.

Sally got to her feet and moved to Morgan's side and grabbed her hand. Morgan looked up at her sister and Maverick's arms tightened around her. She looked back at Miles and Martinez. They were watching Morgan and Sally closely. "You don't know." Miles said softly before rubbing his jaw. "You really don't know."

"Know what?" Morgan stood and faced the two agents.

"Where were you born?" Martinez asked.

"What does that have to do with anything?" Morgan yelled, fisting her hands. She was tired of these games. Pain slashed through her head but she ignored it. Maverick got to his feet and stood near her but gave her space.

"We were born in Port City." Sally answered. "We moved away when Morgan was sixteen and I was seven."

Miles studied Morgan as she glared at him. "What are you not telling me?" Morgan asked, not sure if she really wanted to know or not.

"We found a campsite with a box of documents in the tent, while looking for the cameras. The documents were all about you, Morgan." Martinez said, getting to his feet. "Someone has been looking into you. We found surveillance pictures dating back three years ago, some of your clothes and your current daily schedule. The clothes were bloody and cut up. There was even a DNA report. Were you in a major accident within the last year? The DNA report was dated eight months ago."

"What?" Morgan breathed out. She felt violated and lightheaded as the pain in her head increased.

Martinez held up a shirt. The same shirt she had worn the day of the accident. "Morgan, is that?" Sally gasped.

"That's the shirt I was wearing the day of the accident. The hospital had to cut it off before surgery." Morgan stared at the garment in shock.

"We believe they used it to run the DNA tests." Martinez commented.

"Morgan, your mother was Charolette Elliot, but your father was Alpha Elijah of the Atlantis Pack, one of the biggest packs in the central region." Miles said gently.

Morgan felt her stomach clench as she shook her head. "No." she whispered. "That's impossible."

"You are a very rare creature, Morgan." Miles stated. "There have been no known hybrids. As far as we know, all possible hybrids have been miscarried before eight weeks gestation."

"What about me?" Sally asked quietly.

"We did find a DNA report on you as well. Joseph Elliot is your father. You and Morgan are half siblings." Miles answered.

"Why has someone been watching Morgan?" Maverick asked, moving closer to her. She wasn't feeling so good and leaned on him for support. His arms circled round her.

"As a hybrid, she is an unknown. No one knows when or if she will shift, if she will have some other gift, or if she will just be human." Martinez said.

"The author of the notes in the tent seems to think they could use Morgan to end the werewolves in the area. That she holds some sort of power." Taz spoke up.

"I don't understand." Morgan said softly. Maverick placed a kiss on her head. "I'm not some special hybrid."

"Can we run a DNA test to confirm what we found?" Miles asked her.

Morgan swallowed several times. She closed her eyes and turned more into Maverick. "I don't feel so good." Morgan whispered.

"Morgan?" Sally's voice sounded far away. "Morgan!" Her sister sounded more frantic, and then nothing. Morgan was enveloped in darkness.

Morgan's body went limp. Maverick picked her up and moved her to the couch. "Morgan? Baby, look at me." Maverick brushed her hair out of her face. She didn't respond and she was so pale.

"What happened to Morgan?" Hailey's concerned voice sounded loud in the suddenly silent living room.

"Miles and Martinez just told Morgan that she is a hybrid and that her father was the Alpha to the Atlantis Pack. They asked to do a DNA test." Sally said anxiously.

"Oh, I knew she was a hybrid years ago." Hailey came to stand by Maverick.

"What?" Everyone said at once.

"She was with me when I shifted for the first time. I could sense her wolf that night, but that was the only time. When we were young, a werewolf came to her house. Her mom and the man argued, and he said that she couldn't keep him from his kid." Hailey said, stroking Morgan's hair. "He stopped coming around after Joseph came into the picture when Morgan was five. I tried to teach her as much as possible about werewolves since her dad was one."

"You could sense her wolf?" Miles asked. "Can you now?"

"Not really." Hailey said, looking around at those in the living room. "It was a brief moment after my shift. I haven't sensed her since. She does remind me of a werewolf when she gets angry. She can be pretty scary."

"Is it a werewolf thing to have your eyes change color?" Sally asked sitting on the couch by Morgan's feet.

"What do you mean?" Maverick asked her.

"A few times when Morgan has gotten really mad, I swear her eyes darkened. I called it her mama bear mode." Sally shrugged.

"Yeah, Squirt, a werewolf's eye color will darken when the wolf is near the surface." Hailey informed Sally.

"What do we do now?" Dallas asked. "The news about Morgan's parentage was obviously a shock to her."

"There are a few cabins just on the other side of the tree line. Dallas and Hailey can stay in one and the unmarried men can sleep in the other." Sally said. "There is a path that leads to them."

"I'm staying here with Morgan." Maverick stated. "Even if that means sleeping on the couch. We can talk more when she wakes up."

Hailey and Sally made a quick dinner before everyone left for the cabins. When Sally returned from showing them the way, she went into her room. Morgan was still unconscious, and Maverick was growing worried. He pressed a kiss to her forehead before sitting on the ground next to the couch.

If Morgan was a hybrid, how would that affect them? Would she be hunted? Accepted by the pack? Would she eventually shift? Were the rumors true that she could cause the destruction of the pack?

Maverick was so lost in his thoughts that when a hand touched his shoulder, he about jumped out of his skin. He turned around quickly to see Morgan slowly blinking her eyes. Relief filled Maverick.

"Baby." He breathed as he picked her up and set her in his lap, keeping his arms around her.

"Maverick." Morgan whispered as she buried her face in his chest. Her shoulders began to shake, and he felt her tears soak through his shirt.

He tightened his arms around her and buried his face in her neck. "Shh, everything is going to be okay." Maverick whispered as he rubbed her back slowly.

After a few minutes, Morgan sagged against him. "I'm so sorry." She whispered.

"For what?" Maverick asked in confusion.

"For possibly being a hybrid." She sniffled and snuggled closer to him.

"Baby, there is nothing to be sorry about. You are still the woman I am in love with." Maverick pressed a kiss to Morgan's temple.

"I have such a bad headache." Morgan yawned. "Can we go to bed?"

Maverick stood and carried Morgan into her room and put her on the bed. He kissed her forehead and turned to leave. "You're leaving?" Morgan's voice was higher pitched, and she sounded terrified. "Please don't leave me."

Maverick moved back to the bed and laid down. He pulled Morgan into his arms, determined to protect her from whatever she was scared of. It didn't take long before Morgan's breathing deepened, and her body relaxed. He tried to slide back out of the bed, but she whimpered in protest. Maverick held Morgan close until he, too, fell asleep.

*   *   *

Morgan slowly woke up. She took a deep breath as she tried to bury her face in her pillow. Her pillow was hard but smelled amazing. Morgan opened her eyes and realized she was lying on Maverick's chest. She smiled and snuggled closer to him.

"Good morning." Maverick's voice was deeper from sleep.

"Mmm." Morgan closed her eyes and Maverick's chest rumbled as he chuckled.

Maverick pressed a kiss to her head as he ran his hand through her hair. Morgan felt her body relaxing as she began to doze. She could get used to mornings like this.

"Maverick, time to get up." Taz said from her doorway. Morgan had told Taz he wasn't allowed in her room for any reason, and it looked like he was still holding to that rule.

"Give us a few more minutes." Maverick told his brother. His arms tightened around Morgan, and she sighed.

There were a few moments of silence before heavy boots stomped into Morgan's room. The blanket was ripped off them and Morgan gasped. Maverick jumped off the bed in a flash. Morgan sat up and saw that Miles was pinned against the wall with Maverick grabbing his throat.

"Don't you ever come into Morgan's room again." Maverick growled. "You are lucky that she is dressed, or I would kill you."

Morgan scrambled out of bed and ran over to Maverick. She grabbed his arm and looked at his face. His eyes were so dark, and she knew that Timber was close to the surface. Morgan tightened her grip on Maverick's forearm until his eyes shifted to her.

"Timber, it's okay." Morgan said soothingly. She watched as Maverick's eyes slowly began to lighten. "Miles won't do it again and if he does, you won't be the one killing him, I will."

Maverick's lips quirked up in a smile. He released Miles, who looked more entertained than anything. "Now that you two are up, we need to talk about everything." Miles looked at Morgan. "We really should do a DNA test, Morgan."

Pressure built in Morgan's head again, and she squeezed her eyes closed. Her heart began to race, and she felt like she was heating up. Morgan let go of Maverick and took a few steps back. Her stomach twisted uncomfortably.

"Morgan, are you okay?" Maverick asked in concern.

"I'm fine." Morgan whispered as she made her way to the bathroom. "I'm going to shower. I will be out in a few minutes."

Morgan closed and locked her bathroom door before leaning back against it and closing her eyes. The pressure began to build again. Morgan ran to the toilet and threw up. The pressure in her head faded, as did the nausea. When she was done vomiting, she turned on the shower and stepped in, not bothering to take off her clothes.

The pressure began to build again, and Morgan sank to the ground. This had happened a few times over the years. The waves of pressure in her head would go on for a few days and then disappear. The pain was so bad at times that Morgan thought she was hearing voices. It hadn't happened in a few years.

That wasn't exactly true. After she woke up in the car and Luke had gone quiet, her body had exploded with pain. Her screams of agony were what had alerted a passerby that the car was off the road. The doctors at the hospital had no idea what was causing her pain. They told her that they had to heavily sedate her for several days to help her get past it.

A knock on the door pulled Morgan from her thoughts. She didn't answer. "Morgan? Is everything okay?" Sally called.

"Just a headache." Morgan called back. She didn't try to get up.

There was a hushed conversation on the other side of the door before it opened. Sally slid inside before closing and relocking the door. When she saw Morgan sitting in the shower, fully dressed, she rushed over to her.

"Morgan, what's wrong?" Sally whispered.

"My head." Morgan closed her eyes and leaned back.

"Don't fall asleep here." Sally shook Morgan's shoulder. She knew of her sister's occasional headaches. She reached up and turned off the water. "I need you to stand up and get into dry clothes, Morgan." Sally brushed Morgan's wet hair off of her face.

With Sally's help, Morgan managed to change into shorts and a dry T-shirt. Morgan threw up twice more before Sally opened the door. Hailey and Maverick paced just outside the bathroom.

When Maverick saw Morgan sitting on the ground, he rushed to her side. Another wave of pressure and Morgan closed her eyes. She leaned into Maverick as his arms came around her.

"What's going on?" Maverick asked, near to panicking.

"Morgan sometimes gets headaches." Sally explained. "Considering I found her sitting in the shower fully dressed, it's a bad one."

Maverick's arms tightened. "We should get her back to bed." Morgan was scooped off the floor and laid in bed. "Baby, look at me." Maverick's voice was soft as it washed over her. She opened her eyes. "What can I do?" he asked.

"Stay with me for a little bit." Morgan whispered before closing her eyes again. She felt the bed shift beside her before strong arms wrapped around her. The pain hit again, and she buried her face in her pillow as her whole body tensed.

Chapter 18

Morgan's whole body tensed again, and Maverick pulled her more to him. He pressed a kiss to her neck as she started to relax. Sally had said it was a headache, but he had never seen anyone act like this with only a headache. Something else was going on.

"Is this because of what happened this morning?" Miles asked quietly.

"How would you have caused Morgan to get a headache?" Sally asked confused, then shook her head. "When really stressed, she gets like this. It's happened a few times over the years. Rest is all she needs." Sally grabbed Hailey's arm and they left.

Morgan whimpered as she rolled over. She buried her face in Maverick's chest as she grabbed fistfuls of his shirt. Timber whimpered along with Morgan. He didn't like seeing his mate in pain.

"This isn't just a headache, Maverick." Miles moved to the other side of the bed so he could see Maverick's face. "When you had me against the wall and your wolf took control, Morgan's eyes were flickering when she was talking to him. When I asked her about the DNA test, her eyes nearly went black for a few seconds."

"What are you saying, Miles?" Maverick asked as he ran his hand through Morgan's damp hair.

"I don't know." Miles shook his head. "Do you sense her wolf? I can't, but as her mate, you have a stronger connection to her."

Maverick looked down at Morgan as she tensed again. He didn't sense anything except that Morgan was in pain. He used to only be able to smell her scent. Now he could tell when something wasn't right with her. He figured things were changing because they were getting to know each other more and their bond was becoming stronger.

"No. I don't sense a wolf." Maverick whispered as he kissed Morgan's head tenderly.

"Hmm." Miles studied Morgan for a few more minutes. "I will let her rest. Martinez and I are going to head back out and see if we can locate the last three cameras."

Maverick closed his eyes as he held Morgan. She would periodically tense and whimper. After several hours, she finally relaxed. Her grip on his shirt loosened and her breathing deepened. Maverick kissed Morgan's forehead and she sighed. Knowing he needed to talk with Miles and Martinez, Maverick slowly got out of bed and closed the door softly as he left.

*   *   *

Something brushed Morgan's forehead and she opened her eyes. Sally sat next to her on her bed. "Hey. How are you feeling?" Sally asked softly.

Morgan thought about the question for a few seconds before she answered. "My head still hurts a little, like usual, but overall, I am feeling pretty good." Morgan sat up and looked around. "Where's Maverick?"

"He left with Miles and Jayden to look at the campsite to see if there were any other clues about why the stalkers were watching you. Martinez and Dallas went into town to see if they could find Devon and Jake." Sally stood up and stretched. "Hailey is taking a shower."

"How long have I been out?" Morgan asked as she climbed out of bed.

"Almost twenty-four hours. It's almost dinnertime." Sally walked with Morgan into the front room. She handed her a cell phone. "You should probably call Maverick; he has been worried."

Morgan smiled as she took her phone from her sister. She quickly dialed Maverick's number. "Hey, Sally. Is everything okay?"

"As well as it usually is after a headache." Morgan smiled.

"Baby, how are you feeling?" Maverick's strong voice washed over her, causing her to feel calm.

"Much better." Morgan sighed.

"You sure?" Maverick asked, sounding uncertain.

"Positive. In fact, I feel well enough to go for a run." Morgan got to her feet to retrieve her running shoes.

"Are you sure that is a good idea, Babe? You weren't doing so well when I was there a few hours ago."

"Maverick, I am going for a run. I will be taking the North path. It cuts east before circling back to the house." Morgan said as she tied her shoelaces. "I will only be gone for an hour."

Maverick groaned before speaking again. "Fine, but be careful. We should be getting back around the same time. If I am not home when you get back, call me."

"If I don't, are you going to chase me down again?" Morgan asked as she smiled.

She heard Maverick chuckle before coughing. He cleared his throat. "Liked that, did you?"

"Especially the part where you tripped." Morgan laughed.

"Baby, promise me you will be careful and that you will call me." The light-hearted joking left Maverick's voice, replaced by concern. "Dallas and Martinez went to pick up Devon and Jake, but they could be working with others. I need to know you are safe."

"I promise." Morgan's smile fell from her face as she stepped out onto the porch. She had grabbed the handgun from the table near the door and tucked it into the back of her waistband. "You need to be careful, too. These guys have been attacking werewolves."

"That's why we took the four-wheelers." Maverick said. "But we will be careful. I love you, Morgan."

"I love you, too." Morgan said as she ended the call. Sally had followed her out to the porch. "I will be back in an hour or less." Morgan told her sister before she jogged down the steps and into the forest.

Morgan kept herself at a jog as she followed the trail. She felt energetic after her massive headaches. She didn't understand why. After a normal headache or sickness, she usually felt tired and weak. But at the moment, she couldn't remain still and needed to burn off the extra energy.

Morgan was almost to the bend that signaled the halfway point. The feeling that she was no longer alone caused her to stop. Morgan slowly looked around her. At first, she didn't see anything, but then to her left, she spotted a brown wolf walking towards her.

The brown wolf wasn't the only one there. Seven more materialized from the foliage. Morgan noted that they were much larger than a normal wolf. She tensed as they drew closer. She had no idea if these werewolves were friendly or not.

The unmistakable sound of a rifle being loaded had Morgan spinning around, trying to locate where the sound had come from. Devon stood in a deer blind that she hadn't noticed when she first looked around her. Jake and two other men stood next to him. They all had guns, but Devon was the only one with a rifle drawn up to his shoulder.

Morgan could tell that Devon was aiming at the brown wolf. The wolves were upwind, and she didn't know if they knew of the danger in front of them. Her heart rate accelerated, and time seemed to slow down as Devon's hand began to tighten around the gun.

Morgan took several running steps to her left to block the shot, just as the gun went off. She felt a stinging pain in her side as she drew her handgun. She watched as the other three in the deer blind started to raise their guns. She fired two shots at each of them. Silence followed her last shot. The gun slipped from her hand as she dropped to her knees. Morgan slowly touched her hand to where the pain was. Warm liquid soaked her hand. Blood.

A man was suddenly kneeling in front of her. His face was panicked as he looked at her blood-soaked hand. He touched her face and said something, but Morgan only heard the ringing in her ears. He shook her softly. Morgan blinked.

Her side was on fire. The man pressed on the wound causing pain to rip through Morgan's abdomen. The pain continued to spread through her body. Just like after the accident. Everything suddenly felt like it was breaking into a million pieces. Morgan couldn't help the scream that ripped from her lips.

*　　　　*　　　　*

Maverick cut the engine to the four-wheeler and headed up the porch steps. He was anxious to see Morgan. His phone rang as he grabbed the door handle. Instead of opening the door, Maverick stepped to the side and answered it.

"Maverick, get to the pack hospital immediately." His dad commanded.

"Now's not a good time." Maverick glanced at Jayden. He knew his brother was listening to the call. "Morgan wasn't feeling..." A scream of agony came through the line, cutting him off. Maverick's blood ran cold, and a knot tightened in his stomach.

"It's Morgan." Connor said in a pained voice. "She was shot, and the doctors can't start surgery." Another scream cut him off. "She needs you."

Maverick hung up the phone and turned to Jayden. "Get Sally to the pack hospital as quickly as you can." Maverick jumped off the porch and shifted as he sprinted into the forest.

Maverick pushed himself harder than he ever had before. As soon as he reached the hospital doors, he shifted back to human. When Maverick burst into the lobby, he didn't even bother to stop and ask for directions. He followed Morgan's scent. His anxiety rose when he noticed that her scent was mixed with blood.

Maverick saw his dad pacing the hallway, running his hand through his hair. He barely registered the six visiting Alphas as he ran to the doors where a scream came from. He nearly knocked a nurse over as he barreled into the room. When he saw Morgan, he froze.

She was lying on a table with doctors and nurses trying to hold her still as she tossed and turned in pain. Blood was coming from her side at an alarming rate.

"Maverick!" Morgan cried.

Maverick shoved his way to Morgan's side. He cupped her face, and she turned her head in his direction. Her eyes were filled with pain and relief.

"You can't be in here!" A doctor yelled.

"He is staying." Connor's voice was filled with authority.

"Alpha, this is a surgical room." The doctor protested.

"She is his mate. He stays." Connor growled.

Maverick ignored those around him, he focused only on Morgan. He kissed her forehead. "Baby, tell me what's going on?" He whispered.

Tears leaked from Morgan's eyes and Maverick brushed them away. Her body tensed and the blood vessels in her neck bulged as she fought the urge to scream with the pain. Maverick nearly went into a panic as he watched her.

Morgan clenched her jaw as she tried not to scream out in pain. Maverick was here. That's all she wanted. Maverick wiped her tears away again. The pain finally faded, and Morgan squeezed her eyes shut.

"Maverick, it hurts." She managed to get out before another wave hit her. This time she couldn't stop the scream.

She felt Maverick tense as he brushed her hair off her forehead. "What is going on?" Maverick yelled after her scream ended. Morgan knew he was talking to those in the room and not her.

"She was shot in the stomach, then she just..." The voice trailed off.

"We have tried to sedate her to close up her wound, but nothing seems to be affecting her." A male voice added.

"Make it stop." Morgan whimpered as she curled into a ball before uncurling. She couldn't get comfortable.

"Baby, what can I do?" Maverick asked desperately as he continued to stroke her hair. "Tell me how I can help."

"Distract me." Morgan whispered as she clenched her jaw. More pain ripped through her. She felt like her bones were splintering over and over again. To top it off, the pressure in her head was back, making her feel as if it were going to explode as well.

"Marry me." Maverick whispered close to her ear once the pain started to momentarily ebb.

Morgan half laughed/half choked in surprise. "I already said yes." She forced out as the pain and pressure grew again.

"Right now." Maverick's expression was tight as she turned her face to look at him. He was serious.

"Not exactly the way a girl wants to remember her wedding day, but I'm game." Morgan breathed out. The pain became so intense that she couldn't hold back the scream. The pain was getting worse.

"Dad." Maverick said firmly.

Morgan was vaguely aware of someone moving closer to them. She grabbed hold of Maverick's forearm as he continued to cup her face and stroke her cheek. As the pain grew, her grip on him tightened. Maverick kept his eyes on her. There was a tenderness there but also fear and anxiety.

Their 'I dos' were said, and Maverick pressed a quick kiss to her lips. Morgan rolled to her side, her back facing Maverick and she puked. His hand touched her shoulder while someone pressed firmly on her back. Pain seared through her at that spot, and she cried out.

Morgan gasped as a wave of emotion hit her. She felt Maverick's fear, uncertainty, and desperation. She knew it was his. She rolled back to her back and looked at him. He searched her eyes as if trying to decide if he should say something.

"Morgan, it's tradition to mark one's mate after the wedding, but considering your current condition, I think we should wait." Maverick leaned down and pressed a kiss to her forehead again.

"He needs to mark us." A female voice said softly. It sounded like it was far away, yet Morgan could understand every word. Morgan closed her eyes as another wave of pain pressed on her. *"The pain won't stop until we shift. Our mate's mark might just push us over the edge."*

Morgan gasped as her eyes flew open. Her gaze locked with Maverick's. "If we are going to do this, let's do it right." Morgan breathed out.

"Mark you?" Maverick looked shocked.

Morgan nodded quickly before she cried out in pain again. Maverick glanced at someone she couldn't see, before turning his attention back to her. "I know what marking is." Morgan closed her eyes and took a deep breath. "Probably won't hurt worse than what I'm currently experiencing." she muttered.

She saw Maverick's lips twitch the tiniest bit. He waited for the pain to pass before pressing a kiss to Morgan's neck. Morgan placed her hand on the back of Maverick's head as he placed another soft kiss. Her breathing increased as she felt his sharp canine teeth graze her skin.

Pain followed by warmth spread from her neck throughout her body. *"Now, you mark him."* The voice in her head coached.

Maverick's head was still buried in her neck as he pressed a kiss to his mark. Morgan turned and did the same thing Maverick did to her. She bit into his neck. His body tensed. Morgan laid her head back down as the pain intensified again. This time it continued to build.

Morgan screamed as the pain and pressure grew within her. She rolled to her side again and fell off the bed, landing on all fours as she heaved.

The pain caused her vision to go black for a few seconds before it cleared again. Her limbs were shaking but the pain was gone. Morgan panted as she looked around the room. The lack of pain was a little disorienting. She was on the floor in a hospital room. The only person there was Maverick. He watched her in wide-eyed shock.

"Finally." The voice in her head sighed.

Morgan backed into a corner as she shook her head. *"What is going on?"* She asked herself. *"Why did the pain suddenly disappear and why is the voice still in my head?"*

"I'm not just a voice in your head, Morgan." The voice laughed. *"My name is Sage, and I am your wolf."* Morgan's breathing started to come faster. *"I have been trying for years to shift but couldn't seem to. Especially after that car accident. If I hadn't tried to shift so that you had werewolf healing, you probably would have died. The doctors drugged us so much, I was out for days.*

"I don't understand." Morgan closed her eyes as she tried to make sense of what was going on.

"I think the mate bond was the final push to allow us to shift." Sage commented.

*   *   *

Maverick groaned as Morgan sank her teeth into his neck. Had she just marked him? That would be impossible. Humans cannot give marks.

Suddenly he could feel her wolf. He straightened up as he studied Morgan in surprise.

Morgan's scream seemed to rattle the window before she fell off the bed. She was in excruciating pain, and he could feel it. Maverick barely heard his father tell everyone to get out of the room as another wave of pain slammed into him, and Morgan screamed. Maverick ran around the bed in time to see Morgan shift. Maverick's eyes widened in shock. Her wolf was beautiful with honey brown fur and dark brown eyes.

She lifted her head and their eyes met briefly. Confusion and fear filled her eyes as she started to breathe faster, almost like she was panicking. She backed herself into a corner and whined. Maverick moved slowly so he wouldn't scare her even more.

"Baby?" Maverick said softly. The wolf's head snapped up and looked at him. Maverick knelt on the ground a few feet away. "I know you are scared, but I need you to calm down for me."

The wolf pinned her ears back against her head and she growled at him. Maverick smiled. "My apologies. I shouldn't have told you to calm down. Can you take a few slow breaths for me?"

She took a few slow breaths and whined. She turned to look at her side and her whining increased. Blood was dripping on the floor. Maverick scooted closer to Morgan's wolf. "Look at me, Babe." When she turned to look at him, Maverick continued. "I'm going to walk you through shifting back to human. The doctors need to look at that, okay?"

The wolf nodded and in no time, Morgan lay on the ground grabbing her side. She was pale and tears rolled down her cheeks. Maverick picked her up and put her on the bed as he yelled for the doctors.

"Don't leave me." Morgan begged.

Maverick kissed her lips hard. "I'm not going anywhere."

A nurse put a mask over Morgan's face and Maverick grabbed her hand. In moments, Morgan's eyes fluttered closed. The medical staff frantically worked to stop the bleeding. Maverick looked over his shoulder at the large observation window. Jayden, Dallas, Sally, Miles, Hailey, and his dad looked in with worried expressions. Sally's face was pale with tears rolling down her cheeks.

Maverick turned his attention back to Morgan. She was pale as well, and her hair was damp with sweat. He swallowed hard as his eyes drifted down her body to where the doctors were working. Her left side had a large hole in it. They worked quickly before carefully rolling Morgan onto her stomach and began working on her back, where a larger hole was.

Maverick was emotionally spent by the time Morgan was wheeled into a recovery room. No visitors were allowed besides him. He refused to leave her side.

Once they were left alone, he stood and walked to the head of the bed. He carefully tilted her chin slightly so he could see his mark on her. It had sealed over already, leaving a silvery scar that was unique to him. He moved to the bathroom and looked in the mirror. The mark she gave him was also healed.

Maverick smiled as he gently touched it. He had been unsure if she had actually marked him. Pride swelled in his chest as he returned to Morgan's side. His Morgan. She was officially his. He would never have to leave her side again. Well, he would leave her and Sally with his parents and hunt down whoever shot her, once she was better. Then he wouldn't let her out of his sight. Not for a while.

Maverick spent the night watching Morgan sleep, while holding her hand. Doctor Micheals came in every hour to check on her. He told Maverick that since Morgan had shifted, her accelerated healing had kicked in and she was healing nicely but it would still take a few days. It was weird, Maverick could no longer sense her wolf. If Doctor Micheals hadn't mentioned the fact that Morgan had shifted, he would have thought he imagined it.

Morning came and Morgan still hadn't awoken. Maverick was sitting in the chair holding her hand when the whole gang walked in. Sally burst into tears as she grabbed Morgan's other hand.

"How is she?" Hailey asked as she rubbed Sally's back.

"Since she shifted, her accelerated healing has kicked in, it's just not as fast as a normal werewolf's." Maverick rubbed his face. "She hasn't woken up yet, but she is stable."

Dallas put a hand on Maverick's shoulder. He pulled his eyes away from Morgan to look up at his brother. "She will be okay, Mav."

Maverick nodded his head and looked back at Morgan. "I could feel how in pain and how scared she was." Maverick whispered so that Sally didn't hear him.

"Was that before or after she marked you?" Dallas asked just as quietly.

"I could sense her fear a little before but as soon as she marked me, it was like taking a drink out of a firehose." Maverick kissed Morgan's knuckles. "She was terrified."

"I can't really blame her. She thought she was human, only to find out she is the only existing hybrid. Did she even know she was shifting?" Miles asked softly.

"I don't think so. None of us did. After she shifted, she looked panicked and confused. She backed herself into a corner." Maverick shook his head, trying to make sense of what happened yesterday. "She is twenty-three, what triggered the shift?"

"She is a hybrid. The first of her kind. We now know that she does have a wolf and can shift. She has accelerated healing, just not as fast as a full-blooded werewolf. We know nothing else." Miles answered.

"Is Morgan going to be okay?" Sally asked as she wiped her cheeks. Her chin still trembled.

Maverick stood and walked around the bed, pulling Sally into a hug. Sally wrapped her arms around Maverick's waist. "Morgan will be fine. She just needs to rest." Maverick whispered into Sally's hair. Sally nodded but didn't pull away.

The gang didn't stay much longer. The doctor came in and was frustrated to see so many people in the room. He asked them to leave and to come back in groups of two or three. Maverick retook his seat after scooting it closer to the bed. Holding on to Morgan's hand, he leaned back in the chair and closed his eyes.

Chapter 19

Morgan slowly opened her eyes. Her whole body felt heavy, and her mind was foggy. She tried to rub her eyes, but her left hand was held tightly down at her side. She turned her head to see what had her trapped. Maverick sat in a chair next to her, holding her hand. His chin rested on his chest as he slept.

He couldn't be comfortable like that. Morgan tried again to pull her hand from his. Maverick's eyes flew open, and their gazes met. They stared at each other for a moment before Maverick was on his feet.

"Morgan." The relief in his voice was palpable. His grip on her hand tightened. He squeezed his eyes closed as he held her hand to his lips. "Thank goodness you're awake." He whispered before looking back at her. His eyes were wet with unshed tears.

"Maverick, where are we?" Morgan asked looking around. They definitely were not in her room. This room had white tiled floors, white walls and all the bedding was white.

Maverick brushed her hair back from her face. "We are in the hospital, Sweetheart."

Morgan closed her eyes as she tried to remember how she got there. It was hard to think through the haze in her brain. "How did we end up here? Was my headache that bad?" Morgan opened her eyes and watched Maverick.

"Baby, what is the last thing you remember?" Maverick asked slowly.

Morgan's throat felt dry, and she coughed when she tried to speak. Maverick grabbed a cup off a small table and helped her take a drink. When she was done, Maverick returned the cup to the table while she laid her head back on the pillow.

"We were in bed, and Miles came in. Your eyes were so dark, I knew Timber was more in control than you were. Then the pressure in my head started." Morgan rubbed her temples as she tried to think.

"Do you remember anything else?" Maverick rubbed her hand gently.

"I threw up and sat in the shower. Sally came in and helped me change. You carried me back to bed and held me." Morgan met Maverick's gaze. "Why do I feel so weak?" Morgan asked.

"You lost a lot of blood, Morgan." Maverick watched her carefully. His brows pinched together in worry.

Morgan tried to sit up, but a shooting pain in her stomach caused her to suck in a quick breath. She looked down at her side and gingerly touched it. She was dressed in a hospital gown, but she could feel a thick bandage under it.

Morgan closed her eyes in concentration as snatches of memory came back to her. Running. Wolves. Pain. The need to have Maverick with her. Maverick's panicked expression. His comforting presence.

Morgan's eyes flew open. "Did we...get married?" she asked uncertainly.

Maverick's lips quirked up. "Yes."

Morgan shook her head as she smiled. "For reals? Like we are legally married?"

"Yes." Maverick laughed. "The Alpha was in the Operating Room with us, and Dad was more than happy to do it."

"Alpha? Dad?" Morgan's brow furrowed, then her eyes widened. "Your dad is the freaking Alpha?"

Maverick laughed even harder. "Yes. Alpha Connor is my father."

Morgan shook her head and closed her eyes. She was starting to feel exhausted. "Maverick?"

"Yes?"

"Will you lay with me?" Morgan asked as she looked at him.

"I don't want to hurt you." Maverick leaned down and kissed her lips softly. "You took a bullet to the stomach and were in surgery for hours yesterday."

Morgan scooted to the side and winced. "There is plenty of room. Please."

Maverick carefully got on the bed. He had to be on his side because of how small the bed was. Morgan sighed as she moved her head to his shoulder. With Maverick's arms around her, Morgan quickly fell back to sleep.

"What are you doing in the patient's bed?" A male voice hissed. "I demand you get off, now."

Morgan growled. "He gets off this bed, and I will rip this I.V. out of my arm before I walk out of here." She threatened.

The man huffed but didn't say anything else as he check the machines. Morgan could hear him moving around, but she kept her face buried against Maverick's chest. Maverick chuckled as he pressed a kiss to her head.

When the doctor left, Morgan tilted her head back to see Maverick's face. He smiled down at her before giving her a quick kiss. "You know, its not nice teasing Doctor Michaels about leaving." Maverick rubbed the tip of his nose against hers.

"I wasn't teasing." Morgan smiled. "I was totally serious."

"Morgan," Maverick rested his forehead against hers. "I almost lost you yesterday. You lost so much blood. Please don't do anything that would put you in anymore danger."

"Miss me that much?" Morgan smiled.

Maverick raised up on an elbow as he stared down at her with a fierceness in his eyes. "You are my world, Morgan Storm. I would miss you terribly." He whispered before pressing his lips to hers in a kiss that stole her breath.

Morgan's hands went into Maverick's thick hair at the back of his head as she returned his kiss. Her I.V. line pulled a little on her hand, but she ignored it. The click of the door opening barely registered in her mind, but Maverick didn't stop kissing her. There was a light knock on the door, but still Maverick didn't acknowledge that they were no longer alone.

Someone cleared their throat and Maverick groaned as he pulled away. Morgan laughed which ended in her gasping in pain. Maverick looked at the door before sighing and sitting up.

"Dad. Agent O'Brien. Agent Martinez." Maverick said in greeting.

"How are you doing, Morgan?" Connor asked softly.

"I would say well enough to make out on a hospital bed." Miles winked at her. Morgan felt her cheeks heat.

She held her breath as she sat up. "Morgan don't sit..." Maverick's protest ended when she sent him a glare. Instead, he put his arm around her back to support her as he raised the head of the bed. Morgan breathed through the pain as she rested her head against Maverick's shoulder.

"I'm sorry for causing everyone to worry so much." Morgan finally said, when the spasm ended.

"You're sorry?" Connor asked in disbelief. Morgan didn't know if he was just surprised, or if he was irritated with her.

"Morgan, I know that you are probably in a bit of pain, but can you tell me how you were shot?" Martinez asked.

Morgan closed her eyes as she tried to think. "I was feeling keyed up after my nap. I needed to burn off some energy, so I called Maverick to let him know I was going for a run. I promised I was going to be careful, so I grabbed my gun on my way out." Morgan opened her eyes. She was taking this a step at a time as she slowly started to remember.

"I ran North. I was almost to the turn that marked the halfway point when I felt like I wasn't alone. Something felt off. I stopped running and looked around. At first, I didn't see anything, but then I noticed movement in the trees. A large brown wolf came into view. I knew by the size and shape that it was a werewolf. Seven more appeared. I was upwind and didn't know if they knew I was there, if they were friendly, or if there was going to be a problem.

"I heard the sound of a rifle being loaded behind me. I turned and saw a deer blind. Devon had a rifle to his shoulder. Jake and two others had rifles too, but they weren't aiming them. I knew Devon was aiming at the brown wolf." Morgan paused as her breathing quickened. "Oh my gosh! Did he get the wolf?" Morgan asked looking around at the men.

"No. The wolf was unharmed." Connor said quietly. "Thanks to you."

"What?" Morgan asked. Maverick pressed a long kiss to her head as she continued to look at Connor.

"You moved to your left just as the rifle was fired." Connor said. "You were the one shot, not me."

Morgan blinked a few times as she tried to remember what had happened. She could only remember snatches that didn't make sense.

"Where are they now?" Maverick growled. "We need to find them."

"We know where they are." Miles said softly.

"Where?" Morgan asked anxiously.

"They are two floors down, in the morgue." Martinez answered.

Images flashed through Morgan's mind. "I killed them." Morgan breathed. She began to shake, and Maverick pulled her closer. "I shot them."

"You have incredible aim. Where did you learn to shoot like that?" Martinez smiled at Morgan, oblivious to her inner turmoil.

"He was going to shoot him." Morgan said in a daze. "I felt a stinging pain in my stomach. Time slowed as I saw the others raising their rifles. I pulled my gun and fired two shots at each of the men. I dropped my gun and touched my side. There was so much blood on my hand. Then there was a man in front of me. My vision was blurry, and I couldn't really see him. The pain spread to my whole body."

Morgan squeezed her eyes shut as more memories came to her. No one spoke. "It was just like after the car accident. Like every bone in my body was shattering." She whispered. "The pain kept getting worse, no matter what they injected into me. Just like before, the pain drove me to start hearing voices."

"Voices?" Maverick asked quietly.

"A female voice calling out to me." Morgan opened her eyes and looked at Maverick. "She said the pain wouldn't stop until we shifted, and that being marked by our mate might be the key to push us over the edge."

"Is she the one that told you to mark me as well?" Maverick asked. He watched her in amazement.

Morgan rubbed her forehead. "I think so. She was so happy. She said her name was Sage. She told me that she tried to shift after the car accident so I could heal faster, because I was bleeding out. She was trying to save us, but the doctors put us into a drug induced coma for a week after the accident."

Miles sniffed the air as his eyes darkened before lightening back to their normal hue. "I don't sense a wolf in you. You smell human."

Morgan saw Connor, Martinez and Maverick all do the same with confused expressions. "I don't understand." Morgan leaned against Maverick.

"Baby, you shifted last night." Maverick said slowly. "Your wolf is golden brown with dark brown eyes." He paused for a few seconds. "Can you speak with Sage now?"

Morgan looked down at her hands, Maverick's fingers were intertwined with hers. *"Sage? Can you hear me?"* Morgan suddenly felt stronger and warmer.

"Man, it is nice to be able to talk with you." Sage sighed.

"Holy crap, I can sense your wolf." Martinez said in shock.

Morgan focused in on Miles and cocked her head as she studied him. He began to shift uncomfortably under her gaze. *"Ask him who is father is."* Sage commanded.

Morgan studied Miles. His blond hair was darker than hers with reddish highlights. His eyes were a warm brown color. Something about him seemed familiar, almost like when she was with Sally. Like he was her…

Morgan growled as she got to her feet. She felt the pain of the I.V. as it was ripped out of the back of her hand. She stormed up to Miles and punched him in the face with as much force as she could muster. Maverick grabbed her around her waist and pulled her away from Miles before she could deliver another blow.

"What the heck?" Martinez stepped in between Morgan and Miles.

"You are a liar!" Morgan yelled.

Miles wiped blood from his face as he stared at her in surprise. "Morgan, calm down." Maverick said, and then cursed.

Morgan pushed away from Maverick. How could he tell her to calm down right now. She looked back at Miles before turning and storming from the room. She ran down the hall until she saw a nurse coming out of a locker room.

Morgan caught the door before it closed and slipped in. She found a pair of scrubs that could fit her and changed into them. She took the bandage off her side and ran her fingers over the smooth skin. Not a single scratch.

"With you calling me forward, I was able to heal you." Sage said. *"But it took a lot of my energy to heal you so quickly. I need to step back for a while. Call me if you need me."*

The anger and sense of strength faded. Morgan sighed, suddenly feeling tired. She needed to go home. All she wanted was a shower and her own bed.

* * *

Maverick tried to follow Morgan, but his dad stopped him with a look. All eyes turned to Miles as he wiped blood from his nose again. What had gotten into Morgan? He sensed Sage and then Morgan snapped. She didn't even cry out when he grabbed her waist.

"What was that about?" Martinez asked Miles.

"I think her wolf sensed that I am her half-brother." Miles sighed as he leaned back against the wall. "I wanted the DNA test confirmed before I said anything."

Maverick glared at the man. "Because you decided to not share your suspicions with Morgan, my wife is now running around the day after being shot in the stomach with a hunting rifle." Maverick was roaring by the time he was done speaking.

"Okay. So, I should have told her." Miles said. "I should have learned that lesson from your experience."

"What's that supposed to mean?" Maverick growled.

"That's enough!" Connor yelled. "Finding Morgan is the only thing that matters. I can no longer sense her nearby. Her wolf was pushing forward and taking control. Who knows if she shifted again. Now let's go."

Maverick didn't need to be told twice. He stormed from the hospital room and sniffed the air. He followed Morgan's scent down the hall to a laundry basket. Something blue was mixed in among the white sheets. He reached in and pulled out a hospital gown.

"Either she shifted, or she is running around without clothes." Martinez commented.

"O'Brien. Martinez. You two go check the parking lot to see if you can pick up her scent out there." Maverick ordered as he glared at the garment.

He chucked the gown back in the hamper. He ran his hand through his hair as he fought Timber for control. He needed to know that Morgan was safe.

"You know I would never leave without telling you." Morgan's voice came from behind him.

Maverick spun around. Morgan was leaning her shoulder against the wall as she watched him. She was dressed in a pair of green scrubs and glaring at him.

"I can't believe you told me to calm down again." She seethed.

"I wasn't thinking." Maverick felt his anger calming just knowing she was safe.

"That was obvious."

"Baby, how is your side?" Maverick's gaze dropped to where the bullet wound was.

Morgan pulled up her shirt. There was no wound, just smooth, tanned skin. Maverick stepped up to her and ran his hand over her stomach, around her side to her back. Her breath hitched as he did.

"How is this possible?" Maverick whispered.

"Sage healed me, but it took a lot out of her. She is resting now." Morgan said as she ran her hands up Maverick's chest. "Maverick, I just want to go home."

Maverick kissed Morgan's forehead before pulling her back to her hospital room. He pressed the call button and then gathered their things. As soon as the nurse opened the door, Maverick told her to get Doctor Michaels immediately.

Chapter 20

Morgan sighed when Maverick pulled up in front of the cabin. She was so tired. She waited for Maverick to open the door for her before sliding out of the jeep. He grabbed her hand, threading their fingers as they walked inside.

"Where is Sally?" Morgan asked when she realized no one else was in the house.

"She is staying with Hailey and Dallas tonight." Maverick smiled at her. "They are planning on coming back tomorrow evening."

"Hmm." Morgan turned towards her room.

"Where are you going?" Maverick asked as he followed her.

"I feel gross. I'm jumping in the shower." Morgan didn't bother closing the door before she started to undress. "Are you going to close the door?" she asked, glancing over her shoulder.

Maverick stood in the doorway watching her. At her question, he stepped in and closed the door behind him. He pulled his shirt off as he stepped around Morgan and turned on the water. While the water was heating, Maverick finished undressing. He pulled her into the shower with him before kissing her.

Morgan blushed as she glanced at Maverick while she got dressed into her pajamas. He caught her watching him and winked. Morgan bit her lip as she tried not to smile. If she had thought she was tired before, she was exhausted now. She could hardly keep her eyes open.

As soon as both of them were dressed, Maverick pulled Morgan back into his arms. "How about we get you to bed?" He whispered as he kissed her neck.

Morgan tilted her head to the side to allow Maverick more access. "Maverick." Morgan breathed out his name.

"Hmm?" He continued to kiss her neck. When he got to where he marked her, Morgan shivered.

"I'm so tired." Morgan groaned in disappointment. Maverick pulled back and looked at her. She buried her face in his chest and closed her eyes. She was tired enough to fall asleep right where she stood.

Maverick picked her up and walked into the bedroom. He laid her on the bed and pulled the covers back before climbing in beside her. As soon as Maverick settled in, Morgan cuddled up to him and closed her eyes. He ran his fingers through her wet hair, and she relaxed even more.

"I'm sorry, Morgan. I should have waited till you were fully recovered." Maverick kissed her head.

Morgan laughed lightly. "I'm not sorry. If I wasn't feeling up to it, I would have closed the bathroom door in your face."

Maverick chuckled. "Get some rest, Baby." The exhaustion quickly pulled Morgan into a deep sleep.

*   *   *

Soft snoring woke Morgan. She blinked her eyes open. Maverick had his arms wrapped around her with her back against his chest. His face was buried in her hair. Morgan and Maverick had been at the cabin all weekend alone. Sally had decided to stay with Hailey to allow the newlyweds some time.

It was early Sunday morning and Sally would be coming home that evening. Morgan was feeling a lot better, but her stamina was still lacking. Maverick had called Doctor Michaels yesterday to ask about Morgan's lack of energy. She had become so tired on a short walk that Maverick had to carry her back to the cabin. The doctor said it was her blood loss combined with shifting for the first time. Maverick was sweet and did all the cooking and cleaning. He kept her in bed, resting for the most part.

Morgan rolled so she was facing him. She gently brushed his thick hair off his forehead. His hair was sticking out all over the place. Morgan bit her lip as she smiled. She couldn't get enough of this man.

Morgan pressed a soft kiss to his lips, and after a second, he sleepily returned it. "Mmm. Can't complain about waking up before the sun when that is my wake-up call."

Morgan laughed. "You wouldn't complain either way."

"True. As long as you are in my arms." Maverick smiled before kissing her again.

"Maverick, I'm tired of being in bed. I need to get up."

That had him fully awake. "I don't want you pushing yourself. You've already convinced me to not let you rest several times this weekend. And then you sleep for hours afterwards."

"The pool is perfectly relaxing." Morgan smiled. She got out of bed and walked out of the bedroom.

"Morgan." Maverick called after her several times as she slipped out the back door and out onto the back porch.

By the time he walked out on the deck, Morgan was in the water. She was in the deep end with her hands on the edge of the pool. She hadn't turned on the porch or pool lights and the sliver of moon only provided the slimmest of light.

"Morgan, you get tired too easily to be swimming." Maverick crossed his arms over his chest. "And you are in your pajamas."

Morgan smiled to herself. "Have you never found swimming in the moon light relaxing?"

"I'm not jumping in to save you." Maverick took a seat on a lounge chair but stood up quickly. He picked up what he had sat on. He took a moment to study it before dropping it back onto the chair. "Morgan." He warned.

"Maverick." Morgan mimicked his tone.

She pushed off the wall before gliding through the water, her head just below the surface, to the other side of the deep end. She sat on the step. She kept her shoulders just below the surface to keep the chilly night air off her wet skin. Maverick broke the surface right in front of her, causing her to jump. Morgan hadn't heard him get in the pool. She placed her hands on his shoulders and realized he still had his clothes on.

"You're playing with fire, Baby." Maverick whispered close to her lips.

"Playing? I was trying to fan the flames." Morgan pouted. Maverick growled as he pulled her to him before capturing her lips with his.

*   *   *

Morgan was cuddling with Maverick on the couch watching a movie when Sally burst through the front door. Hailey and Dallas followed behind. "How are you doing?" Sally asked as she eyed Morgan up and down anxiously.

"I am feeling much better." Morgan smiled at her sister. "Perks of werewolf genes, I guess. Sage healed me the next day."

"I only saw a brief glimpse of fur the same shade as your hair." Sally said excitedly. "Can you show me?"

Morgan went to stand, but Maverick's arms tightened around her. "Shifting takes a lot of energy. Are you sure this is a good idea?"

Morgan gave Maverick a quick kiss. "I haven't shifted since that first time. I don't even know if I can."

Maverick sighed as he stood. "Alright. We can also see if you can mind-link."

Morgan stood outside, slightly away from everyone else. She took a slow deep breath. "I have a question." She said nervously.

Hailey laughed. "Okay?"

"Is it normal to only be able to talk with your wolf when you call out to it?"

"What do you mean?" Dallas asked confused.

"I feel completely normal, like I always have. But at the hospital I called out to her. When she started talking, I felt stronger, and I could feel her."

"No, we have constant contact with our wolves." Dallas said.

Morgan nodded slowly. *"Sage?"*

"I'm here." Sage said as a surge of strength entered Morgan's muscles.

"Why aren't you always with me? Why do I have to ask you to come?" Morgan asked. It still felt weird talking to someone in her head.

Sage sighed. *"We are not full werewolf. We have limitations, I think. We technically shouldn't exist."*

"Can we shift?"

"We sure can." Sage said excitedly. Before Morgan had time to think, she was on all fours. The breeze blew through her fur. *"Another thing about us is that I can't ever take full control. You are always in the driver's seat."*

A movement to her side caused her to turn and growl. A dark wolf stood a few feet away. He was bigger than she was and when she growled, he stopped moving towards her.

"Easy, Baby. It's just me." Maverick's voice sounded in her head.

Morgan walked over to him and sniffed; Sage was memorizing his smell. *"This is so weird."* Morgan said as Maverick rubbed his head into her neck.

"You are so pretty." Sally said as she slowly walked towards Morgan. When she reached them, Sally ran her hand through Morgan's fur. "You are so soft."

The sound of a stick breaking caused Morgan's head to snap in that direction. Maverick maneuvered himself so that he was in front of her as she moved in front of Sally. Two other wolves stepped up to Morgan's side and she knew they were Hailey and Dallas. Dallas growled as he moved to stand level with Maverick.

Morgan noticed that both were bigger than Hailey. A deep menacing growl came from Maverick as two wolves emerged from the forest. The wind blew and she caught a scent that was vaguely familiar.

"That's our half-brother." Sage said quietly. *"I know we already punched him in the face, but can I bite him, too?"*

"Maverick, that's Miles." Morgan walked forward.

"Morgan." Maverick warned. *"What are you doing? I can tell you aren't going to welcome him warmly."*

Morgan rubbed her side against Maverick's as she walked forward. *"Sage needs to do something."*

She heard Maverick chuckle as his wolf laid down. Morgan found herself standing alone in front of the two wolves. The reddish-brown wolf lowered his head and whined. Morgan could feel he was trying to apologize.

"Can we talk to them too?" Morgan asked Sage.

"Only one way to find out." Sage shrugged.

"Why didn't you tell me, Miles?" Morgan asked.

The wolf cocked his head to the side. "You are mind-linking outside your pack?" Miles asked in surprise.

Morgan didn't like that he wasn't answering her. She growled as she lunged forward. In seconds, she had Miles pinned to the ground with his throat in her jaws. The wolf next to him turned and growled. Morgan let go of Miles and turned her attention to the other wolf. Her lips curled back as she snarled. The wolf shrank back a few steps before dropping to his belly.

"I wasn't sure if you were my half-sister. My father, our father, wasn't a very good man. He had many affairs, but your mother was the only human. All our knowledge says the chances of you actually being his daughter, was impossible. Hybrids don't exist." Miles said quickly.

"When did you suspect we were related?"

"Not until I saw the report in that tent. I started to think about our similar looks, and it seemed like there was a slim possibility." Miles grunted as Morgan stepped on his chest.

"I guess he has a point. We really shouldn't exist." Sage commented.

Morgan turned back to Maverick and the others. Maverick was standing tall, watching her with Dallas at his side. Hailey was pressed into Dallas as if seeking comfort. Sally watched her with a confused look on her face. For Sally's benefit, Morgan shifted back to human. The moment she did, Sage faded into the back of her mind.

"What just happened?" Sally asked.

Morgan rubbed her forehead with a slightly shaky hand. With Sage gone, her strength seemed to leave her. Maverick was at her side in an instant. She leaned heavily against him, and his arms went around her.

"Everyone inside." Maverick commanded. When Morgan didn't move to follow the others, Maverick picked her up and carried her in. With so many people there and the limited number of seats, Maverick sat in the only available chair with Morgan in his lap.

"Is Morgan a member of your pack?" Dallas asked Miles.

"No." Miles shook his head. "How the heck did she mind-link me?"

"I want to know how she has such a powerful aura." Hailey eyed Morgan. "I have never seen an Alpha cause another Alpha wolf to cower like she made Miles and Martinez."

"What are you talking about?" Morgan asked as she leaned back against Maverick.

"Morgan, what happened with Sage?" Maverick asked quietly.

"She said we are not a full werewolf, so I would always be in full control. It seems I have to call her forward in order to have any werewolf abilities. I asked her if we could mind-link with Miles, I wasn't sure if it was a mate thing or not. She didn't know, so we tried." Morgan shrugged.

"Baby, werewolves can't mind-link outside their pack." Maverick said softly. "And Miles is an Alpha just like me. We are more powerful than normal wolves."

"I don't understand." Morgan glanced around the room.

"What Mav is trying to say is that you shouldn't have been able to speak to Miles because you became a member of our pack from the moment you and Maverick marked each other." Dallas said sitting forward. "High ranking wolves: Alphas, Lunas, Betas, Gammas, have auras that let other wolves recognize their positions. They can also push their auras on lower ranking wolves, Omegas, to make them submit to them. Wolves of equal or higher rank can feel the auras but aren't affected by them. When you first shifted, we didn't sense any of them coming from you. Which is weird, because every wolf has a rank."

"My wolf cowered before you, Morgan." Miles said.

"Does being mated to an Alpha's son have anything to do with it?" Morgan asked.

"I don't have that kind of power. I am an Omega by birth. When Dallas and Maverick take over the pack as Alphas, we will be Lunas. Lunas are the female versions of an Alpha, so we will have equal power to them. But I have never met an Alpha with as much power as what you were putting off today." Hailey stated.

No one could come up with a logical explanation, even after an hour of discussing it. Morgan excused herself to start dinner. Sally joined her not long after. Sally turned on the radio before washing her hands. They kept the volume down as they cooked.

Sally went to call everyone in for dinner and Morgan slipped out onto the back porch. She sat on the lounge chair and looked up at the stars. There was so much she needed to learn about being a werewolf, but at the same time, not everything would pertain to her. She was an anomaly. There was no one else like her. Not even Sage could help navigate these new waters.

"Morgan?" Maverick came outside. He sounded concerned.

"Over here." she said quietly as she continued to stargaze.

"You, okay?" he asked as he walked over to her.

"Yeah, just a little tired." Morgan smiled at him. "It's been a long day."

Maverick lifted her shoulders before sitting behind her. She relaxed against him as he pressed a kiss to her temple. "Well, someone insisted on starting the day at three this morning."

Morgan laughed. "You weren't complaining."

"Just so you know, Miles and Martinez are staying in the cabin again." Maverick whispered close to her ear.

"Are you saying you don't want to swim tomorrow?" Morgan craned her neck back so she could see Maverick's face.

He grinned down at her. "Your sister, brother, and a FBWHA agent are here. We aren't alone anymore, Love. No more of your crazy stunts."

Morgan laughed. "You love my crazy stunts, but I will take into consideration that we are no longer alone."

Maverick pressed his lips to hers and she couldn't help the sigh that escaped her. Dallas and Hailey came out and said their good-byes before heading home. Sally headed off to bed not long after they left. Miles and Martinez went to the cabin. Morgan snuggled closer to Maverick as they watched the stars and talked quietly until Morgan fell asleep.

Chapter 21

It had been six weeks since Morgan was shot and had shifted. Morgan was back to her normal self. She no longer tired quickly, and she was able to return to work. Maverick hadn't liked the idea of her returning to work when she couldn't even do a load of dishes without having to rest. Morgan had been going stir crazy being cooped up for so long.

When she returned, Missy informed her that Diesel had been adopted by a nice family that lived near the ocean. Morgan was relieved to know he had found a home. She didn't have long to enjoy the news because the kennels were once again packed. Her day flew by quickly and before she knew it, it was time to go home.

Morgan climbed onto her motorcycle and headed for the cabin. Even though she was glad to return to work, Morgan looked forward to getting home. Sally would be there. She was healing well and started a homeschooling program two weeks ago. Maverick had messaged earlier, saying he would be home late, but he would be back by dinner.

Morgan pulled into the garage and headed inside. As she entered the kitchen, she sent Maverick a text letting him know that she made it home. She popped her head into Sally's room to say hi before she jumped in a quick shower.

Morgan dressed in pajamas and was brushing her hair when the smell of bacon hit her. Her stomach immediately twisted, and she threw up. She couldn't seem to stop. Every time she took a breath the smell would hit her, and she would start dry heaving.

Desperate for relief, Morgan held her breath and climbed out her window. She sat up against a tree on the other side of the driveway and took deep breaths of the clean fresh air. Once her nausea passed, Morgan tried to return to the house, but as soon as the bacon smell hit her, she was instantly sick again.

She was leaning against a tree away from the house when headlights lit the driveway. They landed on her briefly as the vehicle rolled past her and parked in front of the garage. Morgan closed her eyes as the car door slammed shut.

"Morgan? What are you doing out here?" Maverick asked as he knelt beside her.

"I don't feel so good." Morgan whispered.

"Let's get you to bed then." Maverick reached for her, but she scooted away.

"I can't." Morgan shook her head.

Maverick looked at her confused. "Why not? Our bed will be far more comfortable than the ground."

"The bacon. I can't go in." Morgan felt tears burn her eyes before she felt the wetness on her cheeks.

"Bacon? Baby, what's going on?"

Morgan sucked in a quick breath. She stared at Maverick with wide eyes. She swallowed hard as she tried to think. She had never been regular and with the whole getting shot and becoming a partial werewolf, she figured stress was coming into play. Could she be?

Morgan shook her head. The possibility was there but it was so slim. She even had the IUD. "Never mind. We can go in." Morgan stood.

Maverick got to his feet slowly as he watched her. Morgan wrapped her arms around his neck and gave him a kiss. Maverick had a puzzled expression on his face when she pulled back. He didn't push the matter, but Morgan knew he didn't believe her.

As they approached the door, her steps slowed. She couldn't help it. Her heart rate sped up at the very thought of the stench of bacon. She entered their home and forced herself not to bolt back outside.

Morgan took shallow breaths as she opened the windows in the living room. Maverick watched her but didn't say anything. When they entered the kitchen, Sally was setting a plate of the offensive food next to one piled high with pancakes.

"There you are. I was wondering where you disappeared to." Sally said as she turned to grab plates. Morgan leaned her head against Maverick's chest, praying his scent would mask the smell of the bacon. "You don't look so good, Morgan. Are you feeling, okay?"

"Actually, I am not feeling very well. That sandwich from the diner isn't sitting well with me. I think I am going to go lay down." Morgan turned and walked from the room. She applauded herself for not running.

She closed the door to her bedroom before running to the bathroom and throwing up again. She lay on the cold tile floor trying to tell herself that the smell wasn't that bad, and she was overreacting.

"Morgan, wake up." Maverick's soothing voice said as he brushed her hair back. "Baby, let's get you to bed."

Morgan whimpered as he lifted her off the floor. She nearly cried in relief when their room no longer smelt like bacon. She curled into a ball the moment she was set down. Morgan heard Maverick moving around before he returned to the bed.

"Sit up, Sweetheart." Morgan grudgingly did as Maverick asked. She didn't protest when he pulled her shirt off. She tried to lay down again, but his arm around her prevented her from doing so. He pulled a larger shirt down over her head. "My scent should help you feel more comfortable."

"Where are you going?" Morgan nearly panicked at the thought of Maverick leaving her.

"No where." He pressed a kiss to her forehead. "But you wearing my shirt will keep my scent close, even if you face away from me or go to the bathroom."

Morgan breathed a sigh of relief and laid back down. Maverick joined her and she immediately scooted closer to him. She found herself cocooned in her husband's reassuring embrace. She closed her eyes and started to relax. She needed his comfort.

*   *   *

Morgan was perfectly fine the next morning. Sally even heated up left over bacon and it didn't affect her. She went to work and came back home with no more incidents, even though the nausea had come back by midday. She and Sally were watching a movie when Maverick, Dallas, and Hailey walked in.

"You ready, Squirt?" Hailey asked with a smile.

"Ready for what?" Morgan asked as she paused the movie.

Sally stood from the couch. "I'm spending the weekend with Hailey."

"Why didn't I know about this? Not that I would have a problem with it, but still." Morgan furrowed her brow. It wasn't like her to not remember something like this.

"I told you a week ago." Sally argued.

"We talked about it over dinner." Maverick studied her.

Morgan rubbed her forehead before smiling at her sister. "You don't want to be getting to their house too late, go grab your stuff."

Hailey plopped down on the couch and put an arm around Morgan as the guys headed for the kitchen. "You look a little green." Hailey whispered.

"Just a little flu bug or something." Morgan shrugged.

"You are a terrible liar. You always have been." Hailey whispered even quieter. "Dallas, can you grab my purse from the car please." She called loudly.

"Sure." Dallas was only gone for a minute and then headed back to the kitchen.

"We are going for a walk." Hailey said, pulling Morgan with her. Once they were a good distance from the house, Hailey whirled on Morgan. "Okay. So, I am going to let you in on something Dallas doesn't even know yet."

Hailey pulled something out of her purse and showed it to Morgan. "Oh my gosh, Hails. Congratulations." Morgan whisper-yelled. "When did you find out?"

"This morning. I want to tell Dallas in a fun way. We have been trying for a few years, so this is huge. I am only about eight weeks, so it's still pretty early." Hailey beamed. Morgan smiled and gave her friend a big hug. "I have an extra test I didn't use." She whispered close to Morgan's ear.

"How did you...?" Morgan pulled back in surprise.

"You look as sick as I feel." Hailey smiled as she handed Morgan the extra test. "Taking it doesn't cost you anything."

"But I can't be, Hails. I have an IUD and the odds of me being pregnant are so slim." Morgan shook her head as she stared at the small package in her hand.

"If you were going to just come outside, why did I need to get your purse for you?" Dallas called from the porch with laughter in his voice. Maverick's laughter joined his brother's and Morgan took a deep breath.

"Because I have to keep you on your toes, and you love me." Hailey called back.

"I'm ready." Sally stepped outside as well.

"Enjoy your weekend." Hailey gave Morgan a wink before heading towards their truck. "I better get a text from you tomorrow."

Morgan slipped the test into her pocket before slowly walking to the porch. Maverick slipped an arm around her and waved good-bye to the others. Morgan rested her head on Maverick's chest as the truck disappeared.

"How are you feeling tonight?" Maverick asked as they returned inside.

"Tired and a little queasy." Morgan answered honestly.

"Let's take it easy and call it an early night tonight. Hopefully you are feeling better in the morning." Maverick's concern came through the mate bond.

The rest of the day they spent cuddled on the couch watching movies. Maverick made chicken noodle soup for dinner and then they headed to bed. Morgan closed her eyes while listening to the rhythmic sound of Maverick's heart beating. He absentmindedly played with her hair as he read a book.

Morgan lay awake. She couldn't get to sleep. A soft snore came from Maverick as he slept, and Morgan smiled. He didn't believe her when she told him that he snored.

She was a bit jealous that he was asleep. It was just after three, and Morgan was no closer to falling asleep than when they first called it a night.

Giving up, Morgan slowly slid out of bed, careful not to wake Maverick. She closed the bathroom door before turning on the light. She easily found the test where she had hidden it. Taking a deep breath for courage, she opened it.

Instead of waiting for the results, Morgan went back and sat on the edge of the bed. She couldn't believe she had taken the test. It was ridiculous to think she could be pregnant. She got her IUD less than three years ago.

"Hey, Baby, what's wrong?" Maverick's tired voice startled her.

Maverick scooted to the edge of the bed and sat next to her. He pressed a kiss to her shoulder as he wrapped his arms around her. Morgan's hands grew sweaty, and she rubbed them on her pajama pants.

"Cards on the table?" Morgan whispered.

"Always." Maverick was immediately more awake.

"I left something on the counter in the bathroom, but I'm too nervous to get it." Morgan said the words in a rush.

"Okay? Is there a spider or something?" Maverick asked as he stood and walked into the bathroom.

"Wait! I wasn't done." Morgan called after him.

Morgan's stomach knotted with tension. Her hands started to shake as she waited. Maverick finally stepped back into the bedroom. "Is this it?" he asked, confused.

He held the test but didn't seem to know what it was. The test was a cheap one with only two words on it. 'Positive' was written next to a picture of two lines and a single line image was next to the word 'negative'. Just looking at it, the test could be for a lot of different things. The package was the only thing that identified it as a pregnancy test.

"Yeah." Morgan's voice squeaked. He lifted his eyes from the test and looked at her. "What does it say?" Morgan finally asked.

"Uh, I don't know how to read this. Are there supposed to be words? And I didn't see any creepy crawlers." Maverick flipped the bedside light on and sat down next to her. He passed her the test, but she couldn't look down at it. Her eyes remained glued to Maverick's face. "What is that anyway? Does it test to see if you have the flu or a cold?"

"Cards on the table?" Morgan whispered.

"You said that already." Maverick smiled at her.

"It's a pregnancy test." Morgan barely got the words out as her anxiety climbed.

Maverick's teasing smile slipped from his face. He studied her closely before his eyes dropped back down to the test in her hands. Morgan swallowed several times. She tightened her hand around the test.

"It's nearly impossible, right?" Morgan asked anxiously. "The IUD is crazy effective. The odds are so small that it is practically impossible." Morgan knew she was rambling and procrastinating.

"Baby, breathe." Maverick grabbed her face. He used his thumb to wipe a tear from Morgan's cheek. "What does it say?"

"I don't know." Morgan said. "You are the one that looked at it."

"I didn't know what I was looking at." Maverick laughed. "Even if I did, I wouldn't know how to read it. Stop prolonging this and just look at it." Maverick pressed a quick kiss to her lips.

The kiss gave her enough courage to look down. At first there only appeared to be one line, but in the dim light she wasn't sure. Morgan lifted it closer and tilted it to the light. She was so surprised, she froze.

"Well?" Maverick asked anxiously.

"Is there a second line?" Morgan asked, turning to face him.

Maverick took the test from her hand and looked at it. "There is definitely a second line. What does that mean?" He turned his blue eyes back to her.

"That means we are going to be parents." Morgan said as butterflies broke out in her stomach.

Maverick looked back down at the test, then back up to her. A slow smile spread across his face. Morgan couldn't help the smile that curved her lips as well. Maverick cupped her cheek and kissed her softly.

Now that the unknown was gone and shock replaced her earlier anxiety, Morgan was tired. Maverick turned the light off while she climbed into bed. She lay on her back and stared at the ceiling. Before Maverick laid back down, he pressed a kiss to Morgan's stomach, causing her to laugh.

He pulled her close and kissed her, long and sweet. "You are my everything, Morgan." He whispered against her lips. "My best friend. My wife.

The mother of my child." He kissed her between each title he listed. "I love you."

THE END

The Hunter Guardian Series

The Hunted Guardian
The Stone's Keeper
The Stone's Secret

Other books by this author:

Left Broken
Embracing Dove
Hoodwinked

When Worlds Collide Series

When Worlds Collide
Prey of the Corrupted Alpha

Paranormal Books

Enforcer's Mark

Upcoming Books

Two Sides of the Same Coin

www.ingramcontent.com/pod-product-compliance
Lightning Source LLC
LaVergne TN
LVHW010326070526
838199LV00065B/5670